To Janet
Thanks for hoste...
Best wishes,
Betzy Cox

Dirty Wounds

Dirty Wounds

Dirty Wounds

For Alison

Thanks for all that you teach me

And for always being there.

Dirty Wounds

Prologue

In medicine there are two kinds of wounds. Clean and dirty. Clean wounds usually result from a sharp, clean instrument. It has clear edges, receives care immediately and closes easily. It heals well leaving a thin, barely noticeable scar.

Then there are dirty wounds. They are usually more destructive, often caused by the tearing or crushing or breakdown of tissue. They lay open for the world to see for a long period of time, becoming an ugly wound that festers. It takes a long time to heal and in the process, there are often complications. In the end, the scar is usually ugly, a constant reminder of the original wound. On rare occasions, the wound never quite heals completely.

Those are the physical wounds of life. Then there are the emotional ones. As Kate McCullough knows all too well, most emotional wounds are dirty wounds.

Chapter 1

First impressions can be wrong. For example, someone finding me right now would think I had gotten lost, wandered into a place where I don't belong and had never been before. I am sitting in a dimly lit, poorly maintained, barely inhabited deadbeat bar. But that impression would be wrong. While on the surface, I look like I don't belong, the truth is there is no place in the world that feels more like home to me.

The stools are the cheap wooden kind. Cheaper to replace when the drunken asshole decides to use it to prove his manhood. Or when the guy who should have quit eating the supersized meals about five years ago hears a distinct crack when trying to balance at least one of his two cheeks on the seat top.

The art is cheap print fare, under Plexiglas. Mostly to keep beer splashes off to ensure the pictures outlast the bar stools. Several dingy booths in the back corner. The perfect place for hush-hush conversations between nefarious members of society who think no one has a clue that they are dealing drugs or guns or personal identity information over warm beer and cold onion rings.

I'm sitting at one end of the bar. Not too many people in yet. It is still early. I don't really look the type of girl to be in here. I'm not a biker or a punk or stoner or a meth head. I am pretty much middle class suburbia looking. Probably could easily be mistaken for a soccer mom. Five foot six. Athletic. Years of sports in high school and college left a decent result. I can at least hold my own if someone tries to pick on me. Sapphire blue eyes. My Scot Irish heritage shows in my pale skin. But some other genes snuck into the family tree judging by my dark hair which hangs just below the shoulders. I let it grow sometimes and then cut it back, but never so short as to not be able to throw it up in a ponytail. It's my go to look. Guys have the unfair advantage of short hair or no hair. Thus no issues with bed head upon awakening thirty minutes past when the alarm was supposed to go off. Splash some water on the face and go. Not so for girls. Until the ponytail – it is the great equalizer.

Most would not describe me as dainty or ladylike. I grew up in the post title nine world. Girls can do anything. Truth is, I will always see myself as a chick, a girl, a dive in head first, strong-headed, outspoken, unfiltered opinion kind of girl.

Back to the bar. I'm still sitting on the end stool. There is a skanky looking couple in one of the far booths. Playing pool are two skinny white guys with ponytails, (apparently they were jealous) tattoos that say HATE, and enormous wallets with chains that could protect Fort Knox, holding the wallets to their belts. Like someone would even think about pickpocketing one of them. One, you'd get your ass kicked, and two, there's probably only his lucky two dollar bill and a picture of his grandma inside.

It is a great test of skills to play pool here, what with the tears in the felt and the cue sticks that are worn down to just the wooden stick. No knobby little ending to chalk up intently like you really know what the hell you are doing when playing.

Greg, the barkeep, is cleaning glasses at the far end of the bar. Apparently that is all barkeeps do when not pouring and mixing drinks. I made it easy for him, as I always do. No mixing here. No pretty colored drinks or sugar on the rim or speared fruit added on top. Nope, just straight Southern Comfort with enough of a splash of Coke in it to pretend that it is not straight. On the rocks of course. The clinking of the ice against the cool glass provides a comforting sound that can rock me like a lullaby. That's what I'm doing right now. Stirring ever so slowly, watching the little eddies form and becoming mesmerized by the sound and the sight. I can taste it on my tongue without even touching my lips to the glass.

My reverie is interrupted by Greg. All the glasses must be clean and dry. He knocks on the bar top as if he is asking to come into my room. I suppose it was my own little place down here at the end. The rest of the world shut out.

"Hey Greg." I stop my swirling and tear myself away from the beautiful amber colors.

"Does it talk to you?"

I'm puzzled. My face shows it. "Does what talk to me?"

"The drink. You stare at it like it has powers of divination or prophecy. Just wondering what the Powerball numbers will be tomorrow."

Ha. Funny guy, Greg. Really. He's okay. I can't blame him for poking fun. It is a little weird.

"It speaks to me but coming up short on your numbers, I'm afraid."

Greg shrugs and grins. He's a good kid. At least I see him as a kid. He's actually in his late twenties. Midway through grad school. Thankfully he had the good sense to study environmental sciences so he has a decent shot at a job when he's done. In my book, anyone still in school is a kid. Of course, that means I was a kid up until just a few years ago when I finished my residency in surgery. But now I have a real job, so thus my view on anyone in school.

He's cute and kind. That's good enough for me for a barkeep.

"Kate, may I ask you a question?"

Questions are not my favorite thing, but the category is broad enough that I'm willing to see where it leads.

"Sure. What you wanna know? Megamillion numbers?"

9

Greg gives a little ha-ha. He's easy to be around, appreciates my stupid humor. "Why do you just sit there staring at and stirring your drink? Don't you think drinking it would make sense at some point?"

I stare thoughtfully at the back wall behind the bar. The filthy mirror that was put up when the bar was built years ago is still somewhat reflective through the dingy smoky film and the rows of bottles lining the shelves. I see a cut-off, distorted, hazy reflection of myself.

The image takes me back to another time when that same reflection spoke to me. Not out loud of course but that night, the girl in the reflection told the girl in me to get my shit together. I had lost my brother, lost my mother, lost Scott, the best thing to ever come into my life and was about to lose my career. She said it was time to choose. The glass in front of me or the life I was leaving behind in the wreckage.

I made a choice that night. I make that same choice every day. Maybe I come back here just so that girl in the dingy hazy mirror can remind me of all that I could lose again.

I shake out of my personal little reverie as Greg clears his throat. The thoughts are there but they are not something I share with anyone. So instead I go with a clever quip. "Drinking it would be such a waste of its beauty – its color, its smell, its sound."

Greg scrunches up his face. Clearly he doesn't appreciate this answer. "That's dumb. What's a waste is me pouring it down the drain after you leave every time."

Okay, now he's getting into treacherous grounds with the questions and comments. Why can't he just take a flippant answer and let it go? Truth is, I can't talk about the truth.

"Just trust me on this one, junior. You'll understand one day that sometimes, things are better not being a part of who you are. This drink. It's better all the way around just sitting on the bar with me stirring it."

I don't like conversations about my personal life. People are better off on the outside. But for a moment I actually consider answering more truthfully. That should be my sign to go. Nothing good can come of it. But as happens too often, I don't have the good sense to leave when the getting is good. It turns out, however, that conversations are not the biggest problem for me.

Chapter 2

So right about this time, as I am contemplating sharing more about myself with a guy who knows me as well as anyone, which is to say not at all, the couple in the corner starts escalating. Befitting the setting, the words coming out of their mouths in ever increasing volumes weave a veritable tapestry of colorful filth.

The skinny dudes at the pool table barely look up, but Greg and I stop our conversation as the volume becomes impossible to ignore. Even more so, the tone is what I find deeply troublesome.

"You fucking bitch. I know you are sleeping with him. My business partner. I introduce you and you turn around and fuck him. You're my girl. I own you." Besides rolling my eyes at the cliché, I'm thinking by business partner, this guy doesn't mean a suit and tie, two martini lunch kind of guy.

He is large and menacing and clearly doesn't know the purpose of a comb, the girl a toothpick who may not have had a full meal in years. One swipe and she would shatter like a china doll. She slides out of the booth, tears staining her cheeks, pooling in her sunken eyes.

"I'm not, Joe. I swear to God, I'm not. I..I gotta get out of here. Can't we just talk about it later? Just stay and finish your deal."

With that, Joe leaps from his chair, nearly ripping the booth table off the wall where it was bolted on. "Shut the fuck up Brenda!" To emphasize his point, his backhands her across the mouth. The china doll breaks. She crumbles to the ground with a yelp and a crash. The chairs that she fell onto shutter away, doing nothing to break her fall.

But Joe isn't done. He leans over and grabs her by her stringy tangled hair and yanks. A much louder yelp is followed by whimpering.

Greg has made his way over to the phone by this time. It isn't the first bar fight he's been witness to at the Shamrock. He's wise enough to know machismo isn't good for life expectancy. Waiting for the police is always the wiser move.

Of course, wisdom has never been my strong suit. And there is a woman involved. If two dumbass guys want to have a pissing contest to see whose teeth will stay in longer, let them at it. But this isn't a fair fight. He is twice her size, twice her strength and ten times the asshole. So there I go, diving in headfirst.

Well okay, I do try to be a bit street savvy about it. First I kick him in the back of the knee. A full stomp down with my favorite cowboy boots. Fashionable and practical.

"Get the hell off of her."

He immediately staggers, losing his balance and his grip on Brenda. She scurries away, scooting butt first in high gear. Unfortunately, in his hobbled state, Joe decides rather than chase her he wants to take his frustration out on me.

Since I am a large source of his current frustration, I'm not that surprised by this move and have in fact, anticipated it. A wild roundhouse comes from his right. I am nimble enough to duck it and follow with a straight punch to his chest with my left. Only his reach is longer than mine, so while I barely graze his chest, he grabs my arm and hauls me in. I am now stuck in a bear hug, my face just inches from his foul smelling mouth, close enough to see the nicotine stains on his teeth, of which several have already taken their leave.

13

With my arms pinned between him and me and only the tips of my boot toes touching the ground, I have no option but to begin bucking wildly. With one buck I catch his jaw with my forehead. While that hurts like hell, it does have the desired effect of loosening his grip. I get my feet back on the ground and twist away. But he holds tight to my arm, his other arm wiping his bloody lip.

"You fucking bitch. I'm gonna fucking kill you."

For a moment everything seems to sort of pause. I have one moment to make sure he has gotten my point. "Maybe you should pick a fair fight next time. Only a fucking coward hits a woman."

With that, he punches me squarely in the face. Beyond that it's mostly fuzzy. Me on the floor, Greg's feet. Loud voices then darkness. My last thought – "Okay, maybe not my best plan. But I did make my point."

Chapter 3

"Damn it! That hurts!" I fight the reflex to pull away, knowing the suture needle won't follow my sudden head jerk. Dan had graciously agreed to stitch me up rather than sending in the third year med student, so I really need to be a good patient, for once.

"You should have thought about that before you went smashing your face into someone's fist. What the hell were you thinking?"

Dan is a completely likeable guy. I had liked him in the most intimate way for almost a year before things fell apart. Fortunately he is gracious enough that we are still friends. Good, as we have to work together. He is an emergency room doctor. He's been at Franklin General for a couple of years. Smart brain, gentle hands. I was glad he was on when the rescue squad rolled me in.

That was embarrassing. I'll be hearing about that for years. "Yeah, remember the time we picked up Doctor McCullough from that bar where she had jumped that guy?" Hahaha. I would have made my own way here, but it was only after I rolled into the ED that I started to have sense enough to know which way was right and which was left. Fortunately just a concussion rather than a brain bleed or something else equally as serious.

"You're lucky it's just a lac. Your head CT was clear. Not even an orbital fracture. Or worse yet, a mandible fracture. Your head would explode if we had to wire your mouth shut." He cracks himself up with that one.

"Sure, make fun. But I was just trying to do the right thing."

He blots the rest of the blood away from the laceration and steps back to admire his handiwork. I can feel the swelling and already know what my left eye and cheek are going to look like when I look in the mirror. Hard to hide this shiner, so I better come up with a quip to answer the repeated questions for the next few days wherever I go.

"The right thing involves picking a fight with a two hundred and fifty pound muscle-headed dumbass at a bar? I'm not really with you on that one."

"He was beating up this chick. I just didn't think it was a fair fight, and I wanted to tell him so."

"Oh, and you fighting with him is a fair fight? That's funny."

I punch his shoulder, partly in jest and partly in offense at his insinuation, right as it is.

"I did okay. But maybe I should take Krav Maga or something. Need a better strategy."

Dan bundles up all of the bandages and tosses them in the red bag, being sure to drop the sharps in the red sharps box on the wall. He peels off his purple latex gloves and shoots them into the trash.

"Isn't the philosophy of Krav Maga to avoid a physical conflict? Here's a strategy you could try out, no training involved. Walk away and call the cops."

I try smiling but that hurts like hell.   You never realize how much a smile involves the wrinkles around the eyes until your wrinkles are erased by a huge bruise. I gently probe the wound. A couple of inches just over the outer edge of the eyebrow. That will leave a scar.

"Everyone is a Monday morning quarterback. I couldn't just stand by and watch the guy beat the crap out of her."

I slip off of the stretcher, peeling off the drape towel that was lying over my shoulder. My shirt is a total loss from bloodstains.

16

Thank goodness for a job where scrubs are the uniform. There is an endless supply in the locker room, and they are as comfortable as wearing your pajamas to work. I'll grab a set before I go see anyone.

Dan pauses before he leaves the room. He turns and stares intently at me for a moment. I had had forgotten the intensity of the hazel color of his eyes before. Tinged with a few golden flecks. His eyes say a whole lot, show a lot of life. Not everyone's eyes do that. I get lost in them for a moment.

Suddenly he takes a big step towards me and wraps his arms around me. I pause for a moment, standing like a stiff dead body inside his embrace. It catches me off guard but my brain kicks in, or maybe it is a distant reflexive instinct, but in a moment I wrap my arms around his strong broad shoulders. He's a swimmer, trim body, broad shoulders. It feels safe and nice here. I wish I could go back to this place again.

"It would kill me if anything happened to you, Kate. You are one of the smartest, most talented surgeons and best people around here. Please don't keep throwing yourself into these crazy situations. You can't save everyone, and you are gonna get yourself killed trying."

He lets go. Caresses my cheek for a moment. It was the same hand that had just finished sewing me up, but this touch feels different. But then it is gone in a flash. I blush. I hate when my body betrays my emotions. Emotions I did not know were even there until the red showed up in my cheeks. I thought I had moved on. At least that is what I have been telling myself. Clearly the body has other ideas. I clear my throat and flip my hair back over my shoulder, pull away. Intimate moment over. He deserves better than me.

"I'll try to do better. But you know me – fools rush in…" I added a little laugh trying to lighten the moment back up. "Anyway, thanks for the sewing. I gotta go change and check on some patients."

"I thought you were off call tonight. At the bar and all."

"I am but I want to check on a couple of folks. And I wasn't drinking."

I wave as I slip past him out the door, not looking back to see him watch me walk away, dodging stretchers, nurses, tech and patients clogging the hallway.

Last thing I need is to worry about someone caring about me.

Chapter 4

A hospital is a strange place for the unfamiliar. Hushed whispers, closed doors, bells and beeps, alarms and overhead announcements. Halls filled with stretchers with frail, ghostly appearing figures being whisked up and down the hall. And all the while in the background, there is some laughter and chatter and gossip just as you would hear at the local watering hole. The nurses' station is the heart of any floor. The center of communication. The control central so to speak. But it is also where staff congregates in the quieter and slower moments to catch up, to blow off steam.

But nowhere is stranger then in the intensive care units. Glass walled rooms, like giant fishbowls. Large machines with computer screens, beeps, tubes and alarms. Patients, people looking barely human for all the tubes and lines going into and coming out of. It is into the STICU, the Surgical Trauma Intensive Care Unit that I enter. I stopped to grab a clean pair of scrubs from the locker room on my way up, but there's no hiding the enlarging shiner on my face. Already throbbing.

Michele looks up from her computer as I enter. She's a few years older than me and decades wiser. A great nurse and an even better friend. Her dark hair, dark eyes and petite trim body result in a quiet, understated beauty.

"Damn Kate, what happened?"

She walks over to get a better look at my face. I stand like an injured five year old while she inspects. That's how things work for us. I get into trouble and she is there to play mom and pick up the pieces for me. It is because she is an actual mom, with two little boys

19

that are the joy of her life. The job has meaning and purpose, but it is her kids that fill her heart. For me, there is only the job.

I smile as much as my mutilated face will allow. "Walked into a door?"

She looks at me skeptically. She never buys my crap anymore. Knows me too well.

"Some door. I probably don't want to know."

I slip past her over to an open computer and start clicking away, logging into the electronic medical records system.

"What are you doing here anyway? I know you are not on. I already had to talk to that asshole Bradley three times tonight."

I look up with a sly smile. "Don't hold back, Michele. Share how you really feel about him."

"I can't help it. He is such a pompous little shit. Brand new to the place and he acts like he's the only one who has ever practiced medicine before. A little humility would do him good."

I laugh at her earnestness. Bradley is a new trauma surgeon. The third one on our team. He can be a prick.

"Come on Michele, you know surgeons by nature are pompous asses. We can't help it."

Michele suddenly grows serious, approaches and puts her hand on my shoulder. Normally I would pull away, but she is someone I have grown comfortable with, so I don't even flinch at the invasion of my personal space. "Not you, Kate. You were never like that. You are one of a kind."

That's about all the serious flattering focus on me I can take. "Just give me time, Michele. I was just wise enough to know who to listen to at first. Not anymore. I'm gonna be a bitch someday."

It's her time to laugh. "Yeah, you a bitch. An impossibly hardheaded, stubborn, independent thinker who jumps into everything you shouldn't, but a bitch? Never. Besides if you were I'd kick your tail."

We both laugh now. She's right on all scores.

"So you didn't answer my question. Why are you here?"

"You went off on your ranting tangent so I couldn't answer. I came to check on Davis in three."

"The stab wound guy?"

"Yeah, complete with his own set of guards. They must get bored just sitting here watching him. He has thirty staples in his belly. Not like he's going anywhere."

Michele shrugs. Prison guards in the hospital are a regular occurrence. We are the closest hospital to the state's largest regional jail. We get all of their sick or injured prisoners. They always have to be accompanied by guards. Sometimes one, sometimes two. Depends on the offense. I never ask.

Apparently, Davis is awaiting trial so he has just one guard.

Michele shrugs and goes back to her work. "I'm sure he's staying put, but since last year when that guy snuck down the back stairs while the guard was in the john, they don't even take the time to blink."

"Bet that guard caught hell for that." I turn to go into the fishbowl labeled number three. Curtain pulled to give some privacy.

"Kate, check on him, then get out of here. You are allowed to have some fun in life. Take a night off. Go home and put ice on your face. You are gonna look like hell in the morning."

"Thanks Michele. Love you, too."

Chapter 5

I'll never cease to be amazed at what human beings will willfully and intentionally do to each other. And that is saying a lot because the things I have sewn up, patched up, and cleaned up have been, at times, unbelievable.

In this case, Mr. Evan Davis really was pretty run of the mill. Not all that surprising giving his living environment. He had been brought in the night before after getting shanked in the gut while waiting in line for his dinner tray at Southern Regional Jail. Hence his introduction into my world.

He is a geeky skinny white guy who looks nothing like most of my prisoner patients. Most I would not want to meet alone in a dark alley. If I met him, I think he would be the one to run. My heart usually picks up a couple of paces when I go in to see my post-op, prisoner patients. Not that I feel afraid, just somewhere in my primal brain it realizes I should be, so it kicks in. Or there may be other reasons.

Not with this guy. Not even a skipped beat. I slip around the curtain after knocking lightly on the door frame.

"Hey Mr. Davis. How are you doing?"

He scoots himself up a bit in the bed, wincing from the pain of the effort.

A prison guard sits in the corner, staring at the television as ESPN plays, volume barely audible. He barely looks over when I come in. In the hospital there are so many people in and out of a room that the guards usually get somewhat immune to it and despite best

22

effort vigilance tends to ebb a bit. Who can blame them after hours of staring at a TV or magazine? The guards are always the happiest when discharge time comes around. The prisoners are usually not.

Davis holds his stomach as he tries to resettle himself. "Hurting"

"You are going to be sore for a while. You were knifed in the gut first by whoever attacked you and then by me. My work was much prettier."

He doesn't notice my attempt at humor. Just grimaces

"Let me take a look at your incision." I start to pull down the crisp spotless white sheet and tug at the hospital gown, puke color green with a printed pattern of blue swirls. A fashion nightmare.

It is at this point the guard stirs. He gets up, mumbles something about excusing himself and steps around the drawn curtain, disappearing except for his feet that pace up and down outside the room. Most guards get squeamish and some even respect the privacy of the patient.

Davis's belly is a bit distended. A five-inch incision, angry red with a railroad track of staples runs down the center of his belly with just a slight turn around the belly button. I slip my stethoscope onto the skin, listening intently for any sign of activity in his intestines. Gently palpate. He grimaces but not unusually tender.

I straighten, hang my stethoscope back around my neck. "Looks good. It may take a few weeks before you're not hurting all the time. But you were a lucky guy. The knife missed anything vital. The bowels must have just slid out of the way when the knife went in. Had a few bleeders in the mesentery, which I fixed. You should be as good as new in a couple of weeks."

I have almost gotten to the point in my career as a surgeon that I forget that most people would be freaked out by what I see as a perfectly normal day. In the case of Davis, I got to cut open his belly and play with his guts.

It was my third year in medical school during my surgical rotation that I knew I had to be a surgeon. To stand next to a person and open him up, touch all the organs that hopefully, no one has ever touched before, things that most people will never touch, is amazing to me. The pale pulsating bowels as they process the food, the muscular throbbing heart as it delivers life to the rest of the body, the dark quivering lungs as they send air in and out. Humbling and empowering all in the same moment. The favorite part of my job is being in the operating room.

Davis takes a big sigh, obviously relieved his surgery was over and all is well. "Thank God. I was afraid I was gonna end up with one of those bags hanging out. Nothing was damaged?"

"Nothing important. All you should have to show for it is the pretty scar down the middle and the one where the knife went in. Like I said, lucky."

"Thanks, Doc. I appreciate it."

I turn to leave, pull the curtain back. The guard stands just on the other side. He turns back towards the room at the sound of the curtain's metal hooks on the overhead rail.

"I should be able to move you out of the ICU tomorrow if everything looks good. Probably then a couple of days up on the regular floor. We just need to make sure your bowels are working. They can get kind of sluggish and cranky after I've been in there messing with them."

The guard and I exchange a nod. He has the information he needs out of the whole exchange—how long he and his partners have to take time babysitting here.

He actually cracks a small smile and makes eye contact. "Thanks, Doc." He resumes his seat in the corner and grabs a warm can of soda sitting on the counter next to him.

I turn back towards Davis. "One of my partners will see you tomorrow, but I'll be back the following day. Have a good night, gentlemen."

Chapter 6

Michele is still at the nursing desk working on charting on the computer. Only half of what doctors and nurses do is actually taking care of patients. The rest is taking care of the paperwork. In this case, the electronic "paperwork". For the old time docs, it has been an adjustment, switching from writing orders to entering them in a computer. I sympathize with their bumpy journey into the twenty-first century. Humans don't like change. Doctors are no different. Even when atrocious handwriting makes change a good thing.

Michele looks up as I approach. "You headed out?"

"Yeh. My head is starting to really hurt. Door and all, you know." I give a half smile but even that hurts.

"Uh-huh, door. You're sticking with that? Who stitched you up?"

I feel the flush of heat in my face. "Dan."

Michele sees it. She can always read me. It is her turn for a half smile. "Hmm.. Dan?" She didn't have to add the rest of the question.

"No, Michele. I told you before, it can't work."

Michele frowns, her face grows earnest. "Kate, I don't get it. I get that Scott hurt you. He bailed when you needed him to stand by you, to be patient. Dan's not like that. He wouldn't judge you like that. Besides you're in a different place in your life now."

"I get why Scott left me. I do. I was a damn drunk. But it doesn't change the fact that I opened myself to him. I was honest about who I am and what I've done and he couldn't deal with that."

"I don't know all the details but it seems to me that it was a bit more complicated than that. And anyway, we are talking about Dan."

"I don't know why we are talking about either of them." My teeth clench as my expression darkens. I hate when Michele pushes me.

"I just want you to be happy, Kate. You're happier when you have someone in your life. Just consider it. That's all I'm saying.."

I smile, decide on a new tactic. Try to change the tone to light hearted. "I'm happy. Besides, I have you, Michele. You are the best friend and best person anyone can have." A bigger, kiss up kind of smile.

"Yes, I am. But you know what I mean."

I love Michele. She met me at my very lowest point, going through DT's. She never judged me and always accepted me. But not everyone is like that. People judge, holds things against you. That's just the way people are built. "It's not that simple. I'm bad news. I'll just end up hurting someone. You won't."

"You don't know that."

"I do. I know you Kate. Yes, you are an alcoholic. But you have the biggest heart I know. We all make mistakes. You can't be perfect and no one expects you to be. Except maybe you."

I close my eyes, recalling moments, flashes of the past. "Some mistakes are not forgivable."

A silence falls between us. Michele looks at me intently, trying to read the meaning behind the words. Michele knows me well, but there are some things I can't share, even with my best friend.

I reflexively wipe my eyes but halt mid-wipe, wincing as I hit the bandage over the dressing.

"Damn it. This thing hurts."

Michele smiles sympathetically. "Girl, you're a mess."

I give a quiet laugh. "Aren't I though? I gotta go. I'm wiped out."

"Go girl. Be safe." I head towards the exit from the unit as Michele turns back to her computer.

I turn back as I get to the door. "Hey can you call me in the morning? Just to make sure I don't wake up dead?"

She looks up, shaking her head. "Hon, you are too hard headed for that. You'll only end up dead when I decide to kill you for being so damn stubborn."

She smiles, shakes her head and waves her hand as I grin and disappear around the corner. Neither one of us realizes how close death would soon come for us both.

Chapter 7

I don't get too many days off. Mostly by my own volition rather than an absolute requirement. Truth is, my job as a trauma surgeon at a level one trauma center in an area with a rapidly growing gang presence and generally idiotic people, provides as much work as I want. Mix in some general surgery stuff and I could work every day of my life. It works for me and for the system that is happy to eat up, burn out and then spit out doctors.

But today I am off. It is a day I look forward to and dread the entire month. I wake up early, the pounding in my chest, the images in my head refusing to let me sleep in. I've gotten used to it. Mostly I am just glad that my brain has found it acceptable to limit those things to the one day each month rather than every night as had once been the case.

I slip out of the shower and slip into my favorite soft blue jeans and pair of sneakers. Hair up in a ponytail. A dab of mascara and concealer for the shiner and I am ready to go. Coffee from the Coffeehaus drive thru will serve as breakfast. It is an easy two hour ride up to Blue Mountain State Prison.

I am familiar with every inch of the road by now, having driven it every month for six years now. It is a beautiful winding road up into the mountains. The trees are just beginning to show their early green buds of spring. My favorite time of year, full of potential. The early morning chill is giving way as the sun rises higher, bathing the forests that line the road. Hopefully, I will only have to drive this road for one more year, if things go well.

My mind goes to somewhere from another time in my life. I think about playing on the shore by Lake Paradise. I am seven years old. Bode is thirteen. He's starting to be interested in girls but is loyal to me, his little sis, so dutifully stays with me, playing in the sand. Letting me bury him up to his neck. Nobody really pays any attention to us. Mom and Dad are back in the cabin fighting as usual.

The memories make for a pleasant and bittersweet trip. A time when things were easy and uncomplicated for the two of us. A time when there was all possibility and potential and no guilt or remorse. That time passed seven years ago on a really bad night.

My private world of thoughts is interrupted by the necessity of paying attention to where I am going. I slow to pass through the guardhouse built into the large woven wire fence encircling the prison. I wave causally at the guard and pick out a parking space in the far corner of the lot. The extra walk lets me take some extra cleansing breaths before going in to see Bode. It is the only way I can keep the emotions at bay and retain my composure when I see him.

I make my way through security, an odious task at best. I don't even bother to bring my bag in as it just slows things down. This way, it's just my person that gets inspected closely. The décor of the visitation room consists of grey cement walls and high windows with grey wire mesh. They could at least go for a color. Brighten the place. For the families if no one else.

Bode looks good. Odd to say that prison has been kind to him, but it's true. He has put on some needed weight and has bulked up. He has a full head of sandy blonde hair, a square jaw and soft blue eyes. Not a pretty boy, but someone who could turn heads in the outside world. Next year maybe.

I give him a quick hug and squeeze his hand. As we move to sit, he nods a greeting to a fellow inmate who is sitting nearby talking to a well-groomed young man in a suit. Lawyer no doubt.

"Making friends?" I nod in gesture over to the older, gray haired prisoner who now gives me a half smile and a slight nod. I hold his gaze for a moment. It is not clear which one of us is more curious.

Bode's warm smile brightens the cold cement that seems to suck all of the warmth out of the room. "Him? Yeah. Well sort of. It's good to have friends here. Looks harmless but that guy has some serious influence here."

I can't help but smile and shake my head. That's Bode. Makes friend and wins over people with his easy going and genuine personality. Most people can't help but like him, so there is no reason to be surprised it is the same here. "Always in with the popular crowd, I see." I can't help but think making friends with convicted felons isn't the safest social circle. Despite my effort to keep it light, my concern apparently shows.

"It's all good, Kate. White-collar crime guy. Not like he's gonna shank me in the prison yard." Bode laughs a bit at this. I don't.

"Not funny, Bode."

"Enough about me sis. You look like hell. When are you gonna start taking care of yourself?"

"I don't know what to do with such flattery." I smile weakly knowing I am about to say a lie, a harmless white lie designed to protect, but a lie nevertheless. "Seriously, I am taking care of myself Bode. I've just been working a lot. But everything else is good."

The generous helping of concealer I put on had muted the black eye, but there is really no hiding that from him. He points at it.

"Let me guess, a demented old guy slugged you in the face?"

I give a hardy laugh. "Something like that."

He doesn't believe me but doesn't push it. He's always taken care of me without questioning too hard. It hasn't always worked out well for him. And I carry the guilt of that every day.

"What's going on with you, Bode? You doing okay?"

31

We sit at one of the little tables in the corner of the visitation room. He is not a violent offender so we are allowed to meet here rather than behind glass. He holds my hand. Like it is a lifeline to the real world.

"Good. I've solved the mysteries of black holes, and now I have turned my powers of thought to addressing the healthcare crisis. I thought you'd appreciate that." Always a wise ass. One of the many things I adore about him.

"Oh good. Make sure you set me up in a good spot when you redesign the system. Some position with omnipotence to fix all the stupid people. That alone would save a fortune."

It's his turn to laugh. A deep full bodied voice that instantly transports me back. Him screaming for help. Standing over the man while I stumble around incoherently. I shake my head like resetting the image on an Etch A Sketch.

A moment of silence passes between us. There is so much that has never been said. That never will be. He has never blamed me. He has never called me out for being selfish and stupid. He has never begrudged my going on to finish residency and become a successful doctor while he passed his days locked in a four by six cell. But he doesn't have to. I have had all of those conversations with myself.

"Kate." He squeezes my hand.

I look away for a moment. I need to regain my composure. We don't speak of or share the emotions of that night. Not since the day the guilty plea was filed, when I argued with his lawyer that I should be the one going to prison. In the end I sat wordless and motionless in the back row of the courtroom when the judge accepted Bode's guilty plea and sentenced him to ten years in prison for manslaughter. I watched silently as they handcuffed him and led him off to prison. At that moment, I entered my own prison as well. The biggest difference being that he would be paroled one day. I would remain in my self-imposed prison of guilt and punishment forever. And we never talked about it, not really.

Neither one of us can afford to let that emotional monster out, not here, not yet. Maybe one day when he is out. Maybe then he will scream at me, about how stupid and selfish I was. About how he will forever suffer for protecting me from consequences I deserved. I wish he would scream and yell. Maybe it would let my demons loose so as not to torture me every day.

"Sis. Kate. Hey."

Bode's steady voice and gentle squeeze of my hand brings me back from my darkness.

"Where did you go?"

My eyes well with tears. I turn away. Pull my hand back to brush away the tears, hoping he doesn't notice.

I look back, hold his gaze in mine. He is so strong, so brave, so kind. He knows where I was and without a word we communicate a lifetime.

He reaches out to pull both of my hands back towards himself, holds them out, examines them, front and back. Then he squeezes them with his own. Gently bends down to kiss them.

"These hands heal, Kate. They save lives. That would not be true if things had been different. Everything is as it should be. You have to know that. I am okay. And you need to move on. You deserve happiness and love and laughter. Stop punishing yourself. I took the punishment. You don't have to as well."

I bow my head. I can't speak. I can't look at him. Not without all the anguish and shame pouring out in a tidal wave of dark emotions. I can't let him see it, not here, not now, not ever. But he feels it without my saying a word. We will always be connected in a way that knows no sense of time or space or boundary.

I clear my throat, compose myself. Close the door on those raw and wild monsters that roam my soul.

"I am happy... or trying to be. Really."

He looks at me, disbelieving.

"I even have a blind date tomorrow night." Or probably, since I am on call and so plans are subject to change. But I don't tell him that.

He smiles and it feels like the sun suddenly came out in the room. "Good. Go. Have fun. Enjoy yourself. Let your guard down and let him in. "

I laugh, wipe my face with my hands, drained from the emotions.

"It's just one date. We'll see where it goes."

"Kate, it's okay to let people in and to let them care about you. That is what life is about."

I hold his gaze in mine for a moment then with a bitter and wry expression say, "Yeah right, see how well that worked out for you."

Chapter 8

Life is about the evolving struggle between the mind and the brain. It is a fierce battle at times.

Having left the emotional thunderstorm that is visiting my brother in prison, I do what I have always done. I stop at the nearest bar. In this case it is a little country watering hole a couple of miles from the prison. Near shift change at the prison, I usually find a little cadre of guards unwinding and sharing stories.

The brain is an amazingly intricate web of dendrites, glial cells, astrocytes, Schwann cell, intercellular cytoplasm and such. It is also amazingly simple in that it has evolved to focus on the survival of itself. It instantaneously alerts to any threats to the body and itself and mobilizes all possible resources to protect from that threat, real or imagined. Over time, these responses become patterns of neurons. Superhighways of electrical activity that results in behaviors that decrease pain and avoid injury. Even if those behaviors are ultimately not helpful.

The mind is supposedly man's higher power. Our ability to overcome the brain's patterned responses and to thoughtfully analyze a situation and make volitional choices for the overall good, sometimes the good of itself, sometime the greater good at the expense of itself.

Stopping at this bar is to engage in mind versus brain. It has not always been the case. The sensible and logical thing for a person to do after a tragic accident involving alcohol would be to stop drinking. That was not me.

I had a problem with alcohol before the accident and those brain patterns that made it true did not crash and burn in that moment. By problem, I mean a nice euphemism for being an alcoholic. Ironically, after the accident I actually managed to go from drinking too much at social events to drinking for any reason I could think of. When I was happy, I drank. When I was sad, I drank. When I was bored, I drank. When I was angry, I drank. When I had no excuse to drink, I drank.

Alcoholism is a funny disease. It is a disease and it's not. It is seen both as a biological illness and a character flaw. I had all the genes that created the predisposition. It is a family legacy. But I chose to live up to it. I found out that the alcohol could make me feel less afraid, less hurt by others, less vulnerable to the pain that comes with relationships. So I used it to cope until I no longer knew another way to cope. I used it to keep my brain happy even when things were okay. Just because it seemed to make my brain feel even more okay.

So it was no surprise really what happened that night. The tragedy started when my mind thought it could outsmart my brain. My mind lost that night. And it lost for many nights after that. I drank and drank and drank, trying to erase the memory, the very fact of the existence of the events of that night. It did not work. What it did result in is my getting kicked out of my surgical residency, referred to a substance abuse program and long term substance abuse monitoring once I was accepted back into another program.

It was only when my career as a surgeon was threatened, when I realized I would lose the only opportunity I had to atone for that night, that I realized that I was not in control. I vowed to change that one day. And I make a stand every time I walk into a bar. It is a call out to my brain to engage in an epic battle. My mind versus my brain. My fierce determination to stare down the roaring impulse to pick up the beautiful, calming, smooth whiskey. To prove that I am in control of my brain.

So here I am again, sitting at the bar, staring into the crystal ice floating in the amber liquid. These days are the hardest. The screaming in my brain to just take one sip to drown out the voices of all those around me. But the knifing pain of guilt searing through my heart and soul keep me paralyzed, hands wrapped around the glass, arm refusing to move. After thirty minutes, I can take no more. I pay my bill and head for the door.

I never notice the couple of guys in the far corner whispering conspiratorially, occasionally glancing my way. I never hear them talking about making their move tomorrow night, how the plan is working out perfectly.

Chapter 9

At the end of every day at the hospital I have to take twenty or thirty minutes to review and sign all of my medical notes and orders. Even on an electronic medical record system, the paperwork takes up a disproportionate amount of time for the practice of medicine. Not only do I sign my notes, I have to sign every order for Tylenol, walking, Ensure supplements (including flavor), special pillows, etc. If you go to the drugstore, anyone, all non-medical professionals, can buy this stuff. But in the hospital, the patient may not have it or be given it without making the doctor provide an order for it. Silly. But it's part of my job.

So I am sitting at the surgical floor nursing station doing just this. I just finish clicking on my last note when Michele walks up.

"Busy day?"

I sign off the computer and push back from the desk.

"Not so far. I gotta run. I have a blind date I need to get ready for."

Michele cocks her hip and her head and gives me a look of annoyance and disgust.

"A blind date? Tonight?"

"I thought you'd be happy. I'm getting out."

"Getting out on your damn call night. You really think you are not going to be called back in here twenty minutes into the date? What were you thinking?"

I am a bit sheepish. She is right. I knew that was likely when I made the plans. This suddenly occurs to her too. She shakes her head in disbelief and irritation.

"What am I going to do with you? You don't even give yourself a fair chance of meeting someone. You sabotage every chance you have for happiness. I don't get it."

I put my arm around her shoulder, trying to console her. I don't like for her to be sad, especially for me. "Michele, it's okay. Maybe it will be fine. If not, I'm sure he'll give me a second chance. He is a county sheriff's investigator. He knows what it's like to have a job that consumes your life."

I look her straight in the eye and smile. She reluctantly smiles slightly.

"Fine. Just promise me you will be open with him and be yourself. Don't try to scare him off in the first five minutes."

"Me? Ha, never."

Chapter 10

Most people who know me from work think that I am only capable of wearing scrubs or other casual clothes, like jeans or khakis. I don't dress up and I don't dress daintily.

But I am capable of it when the circumstance arises. And a date is just such a circumstance. So into the quiet, candle-lit, Italian restaurant I totter, in my black pencil skirt, soft lavender-colored silk blouse and three inch, black pumps. A pair of dangly earrings complete the look. My heels clack as I hit the tile entryway. I'm hurrying since I am late, as usual.

Mike Morgan, my date, is sitting in the entryway, dutifully and patiently waiting for my arrival. He stands up as I enter. We've not met before, but he has a description of me, and me of him, from our mutual friend, the set-up person. Mike is about six feet tall, trim, with close-cropped hair and a goatee. Just a touch of grey in the goatee of sandy brown hair. Gentle green eyes, intense, the kind that seem as if they can see into your soul when he looks at you. A nice smile. Strong wide hands with neatly trimmed nails. I have a thing for hands. I like clean and strong ones with just a little hair on the back. His are perfect.

Okay, credit to the set-up guy for good taste. Surprising since it was a guy.

"Kate?'

"Yes, you must be Mike."

I reach out my hand to shake his. Firm grip. Holds a bit longer than I expect but I like it.

"Let's get a table. I'm starving."

He points the way and falls in step behind me. The place is a tiny mom and pop Italian place. Original Italian food, not the kind that comes out of the chains. Quiet, clean, dark carpet and prints of scenes from Italy on the walls. The maître de leads us to a table in the far corner, quiet. Although there are only a few other couples in the place anyway, so it is all quiet.

I slip into my seat and pull the cloth napkin across my lap. Eagerly open the menu. The awkward opening moments of a blind date.

Mike doesn't open his menu; he just looks intently at me, watching me. I feel his gaze and look up. A sheepish smile. "Sorry, I tend to be all business all the time."

"No problem. We might as well get the food ordered and then we can relax. Do you want a bottle of wine?"

"Uh, no thanks. Actually, I should've warned you, I am on call tonight and might get called in. I'm sorry. There was just no other good nights this whole month."

"No, no. Don't apologize. I appreciate you squeezing me in. We'll just say a prayer that everyone in town is safe and healthy tonight."

After I order the chicken carbonara and he orders their legendary lasagna, we sit back over glasses of ice water with lemon to talk.

Mike takes a sip and then dives in. "So you met Brian through the ED?" Brian was the set-up guy.

"Yeah, he brought in the very first trauma I did after I started working here. Really nasty one. Teenaged gunshot wound to the face. Gang stuff. I was really impressed how Brian handled things in the field and got him in so quickly."

41

"Yeah, he's one of the best medics I've ever seen. We responded to a lot of calls together back when I was still in uniform. He was my partner's best friend so we started hanging out socially too. Don't see him so much anymore. Now I show up after the wounded are gone, but before the stiffs are hauled off."

"So do you like being an investigator rather than in uniform?"

"Definitely. Clothes are more comfortable." He flashes a grin. His eyes dance when he smiles but there is a fleeting glimpse of something darker, like the levity is more for his sake then mine. A distraction from the place his mind was going. It's gone in a flash as he continues. "Cop work can be depressing. You see the shitholes of the world, but it is doing something good. Protecting people, helping people. Cliché, I know but it's true."

"I can appreciate that. The world needs more good guys."

I used to really be into cops. Something about a good guy with a badge and a gun turned me on. That changed after the accident. I can't say they are the enemy now. I just get a little knot in my stomach when one is around. So this date is going out on a limb.

But the way Mike looks at me, right in my eyes, as though he can read my thoughts and really see me, does something. I feel drawn in rather than wanting to run away. There is definitely a spark of electricity. I start to relax a bit; maybe I can be myself with him.

An awkward moment. I hate small talk. And blind dates. But Mike plows ahead, unfazed and totally comfortable. "Do you like being a doctor?"

That's a grounder. I can handle that. "Yeh. I do."

"Why?" His expression conveys that he really is interested in the answer, not just in moving the conversation along. I am really liking this guy.

"Lots of reasons. I love doing surgery, for one. But more it is the way I can connect with people. There is something so humbling and so cool about being invited into a person's most intimate, frightened and personal space. To be there while someone deals with life altering news. To be able to provide comfort and encouragement. I don't know. I guess it fills my soul. Corny as that sounds."

Mike cocks his head thoughtfully, as if processing and reflecting on my answer. "What about when things aren't good? Isn't it hard to share the bad news?"

"You tell me. You do it as much as I do. It is never easy to tell someone that they or someone they love is dying or dead. There is so much raw emotion that pours out. I guess we all develop a little detachment from it. Otherwise we would drown in it."

"Yeh. It is a fine line between caring and caring too much. The lines can get blurry sometimes. Detachment makes it possible to do the work. That's for sure."

I take a sip of water as the waitress delivers salads and bread. My mouth is dry from nervousness. But in some manner, it feels like a good nervousness. An excitement more than a fear.

"Let's change to a less depressing topic." I stab a forkful of lettuce and chase a cherry tomato around the plate for a moment. With my luck, I expect it to squirt across the table and hit him in the eye. It doesn't happen. Maybe my luck is changing.

A brief moment as we each take a bite. I press on. Small talk isn't my strong suit but something about this guy intrigues me. "So you said Brian was friends with your partner. Who's that? Maybe I know him. I see a lot of you guys in the ED. I'm kind of surprised I haven't seen you around before now."

By his reaction, I quickly realize that the less depressing topic is not so much that. He puts his fork down, sighs heavily as if weighing the options.

I take the moment to try to backpedal to somewhere less uncomfortable. "I'm sorry, did I bring up a sore subject?"

His gaze holds mine. It feels like our souls spark together for a moment. "No. No. You couldn't know. It's okay. It's history. Just not a happy one."

I look down at my place as I stab a fork full. My effort to let him off the hook. To hide himself away. But he doesn't. He continues on. "Chase Blackman. He was my partner when I was in uniform. We came out of the marines together. Served in Iraq together. "

I look up again. His face is thoughtful, a mixture of happy memories and terrible anguish. My expression encourages him on.

"We survived that hell hole just for him to be blown away by a fucking jacked up crack head."

Silence follows. How do you respond to such a thing? My mind stumbles around looking for the words that weren't cliché, weren't trite. There wasn't much. "I'm so sorry Mike." was the best I could manage.

"You know, lots of people have said that to me. Most of them just say it because they don't know what else to say. They just want the conversation to end. They don't get it." His gaze again holds mine as the moment seems to slow to a crawl. "Not you. I don't get that from you. You're the real deal Doc."

I give a half smile, curiosity, embarrassment, discomfort, all mixed within. "Thanks?"

"No really. Losing Chase was losing my best friend. Like losing a piece of myself. I held him in my arms as he took his last breaths. It was the worst day of my life. You've been there with people, when someone faces that moment. You understand it, can feel it. It just shows on your face."

I look away, his stare bores into me, into places I try to hide from everyone. I feel drawn to him, reunited souls from another time. I want to comfort him, to ease his suffering. Of course, it is what I do, so can I really be surprised by this? But somehow, it feels like more. And that makes me a bit uneasy.

Chapter 11

"I'm sorry, now I'm making you uncomfortable." Mike grabs his fork and makes quick work of the rest of the salad as the waitress arrives with the main course.

We let her distribute the steaming plates and collect the salad plates in silence. But it is a comfortable silence. Two people just being in each other's presence without the need for noise, for chatter.

As the waitress heads towards the kitchen, dirty plates piled in one hand, a server's folding tray in the other, I break the silence. "Mmmm, looks good. So let's make a deal. Okay?"

Mike nods his agreement. "Okay, what's that?"

"No more apologies. We've said sorry like four or five times now."

"Deal." He dives into his lasagna as I tackle the chicken. "You must be a great doctor."

"Why would you say that?"

"Because you're easy to talk to. I just met you and here I am sharing my deepest traumas."

"I don't know about that. Maybe I'm just pushy."

"Not at all. It's just... it's well... how do I put this? It's just feels very comfortable with you."

At this I can feel the heat come up in my face. It's clearly a compliment. One that I find surprisingly welcome. Nothing worse than a one way attraction. And since I know I am attracted to him, it's encouraging to think the feeling may be mutual. Unfortunately, the swirl of hopeful emotions leaves me at a loss for words.

46

Mike provides a way out of the moment. "You know what, how about less intense for a bit? So what do you like to do when you aren't working?" Now that shouldn't be a hard question. But for me it sort of is. I work. That is what I do. It is who I am. It is how I earn some little piece of redemption every day.

"Ummm." I stick another forkful in my mouth buying time. Okay. So given a moment I can come up with some things. "I like to hike. I work out. It keeps me sane. I do my laundry, shopping and house cleaning." I give a grin with this last sentence. Funny, but it's true. That's what I do on my off days.

"Hiking? I love to hike. Are you a day hiker or an overnighter?"

"Well overnight implies two days off in a row."

Mike laughs. A good authentic belly laugh. "Come on now, you have to have more than one day off at a time."

His laughter is infectious and I join in. "Okay. Okay. I do. And yeah, I like the occasional overnight, let's get lost in the woods adventure."

A gleam flashes in his eye. "Hm. I think I'd enjoy getting lost in the woods with you."

I blush. I can't help it. And I can't hide it. And strangely, I like it.

I clear my throat. "Well then. I'm not sure how to respond to that. Was that an invitation?"

He is intently looking at me. I want to meet his gaze, but I find myself unable. I look briefly but then look away. It feels like he could see straight into my soul if I let him. And unexpectedly, I find a part of me wants to. I take another sip of water just to be doing something.

"Maybe," he says as I look up over my water glass. Our eyes lock and hold there. A whole conversation in silence seems to occur in an instance. Only his wink breaks the connection.

47

His smile and the wink, combining to make his expression that of a mischievous teenager instigates a laugh. Graceful as ever, I start to choke on my water trying to suppress it. With desperation I try not to spew it all over the table. He sees my distress and delights in making it worse by laughing at me.

The coughing sets in as I manage to get the last sips of water down. It is only aggravated by the fits of laughter that are now bursting forth. Finally I compose myself enough to speak. "Oh nice. I sit here choking to death and you're laughing. What kind of cop are you? Protect and serve, my ass."

This only serves to make him, and me, laugh harder. The only other couple in the place looks over and smiles, enjoying the enjoyment of others. Tears are coming down my face by this point. What a great impression I am making.

"Okay. Okay." Mike puts forth effort at controlling himself. "I promise, if you are ever in desperate need, I will be the first one there to save you."

I smile. I like the idea. And I believe he really means it. "And I promise, if you are bleeding to death in a heap somewhere, I will stitch you back together."

He suddenly drops his fork and sticks out his hand to shake mine. I grab his in return and we give one hard shake. "Deal. I might have to a have a minor accident just so I can get your hands on me. Nothing life threatening of course."

"So no CPR, no mouth to mouth, I guess." I feign disappointment.

"Well, if you put it that way, maybe something kind of serious."

"Nah, you don't have to go to that much trouble to get my lips on yours." Oh my God. I can't believe I just said that out loud. I double down on the blushing.

There is no way to describe the grin on Mike's face. I scratch the back of my neck, a little sheepish over my lack of restraint. Not that it is a problem for him. Just unsettling for me as it is so out of character. I can't explain or understand the effect this man is having on me. And I can't even blame the wine.

But before we can see what comes next, it all comes to a screeching halt at the sound of my cell phone ringing. I throw my head back, roll my eyes. Of course, just when I was wanted to actually stay for the whole date, and then some, I get called. Damn it.

"McCullough."

I pause, listening to the voice on the other end.

"How far out?"

An answer.

"Okay, I'm on my way. Be there about the same time."

I click off my phone and stuff it into my purse. Scoot my chair back. Mike scrambles to get up to help me. "Don't. Stay put and finish eating. Pedestrian versus car. Car won. I'm sorry."

"No, no. You do what you need to. Can we finish the conversation in the near future?" His grin lights up his whole face and makes me smile too.

I lean over and kiss him on the lips. Just a quick peck, but a kiss nevertherless. I do it before I even realize what I am doing. It is as if the primal instinct in my brain takes over to finish the conversation without words. And it is nice.

"Definitely."

Chapter 12

A kiss? What the hell was I thinking? Banter is one thing. Actually kissing him takes it to another level. I'm obsessing over this as I get in my ten-year-old, beat up Jeep Cherokee and hurry back to the hospital. I'm not a first date kiss kind of girl. Hell, it wasn't even a full date. It was an eighth of a date and I'm pecking him on the lips. It was an impulse. And try as I might, I can't quite get a handle on where in my brain that impulse came roaring out of. Maybe it is my impulse to rescue. There was something vulnerable and broken in him as he talked about his service. Or maybe it is just that I am always a bit emotionally raw for the few days after I see Bode. So I decide to attribute it to that fact.

But now I have to put all of that aside and concentrate on the task at hand – saving a life.

My clacking heels echo through the mostly empty halls as I head straight to the emergency department. The hospital starts to get pretty quiet in the evening. Everywhere except the ED of course. That is an area of controlled chaos. A cacophony of noise and smells and sounds.

The secretary points towards Trauma Bay Two. "In there, Dr. McCullough"

Behind the curtain, there is a cluster of personnel busily performing their assigned tasks over the patient. He appears to be mid-forties. Still strapped to the backboard, wearing the cervical collar that the EMT's put on. His face is bloody. Dan is leading the show. He looks up as I enter.

"Wow, I didn't know trauma was going formal now. I'm feeling a bit underdressed."

I shoot him a look as he laughs, as do the others.

"Is that silk?" Lorraine, one of the most experienced and skilled nurses in the ED chimes in. "Blood stains are gonna be hell on that."

I ignore their teasing and focus on the patient.

"What do we have?"

Dan turns back to evaluating the patient, done with his fun for now. "Hit by minivan. Tossed about twenty feet onto pavement. Glasgow is six."

Three quarters of what we do in medicine is mostly common sense and common knowledge. But we spend years learning the special language that has become the world of medicine. We couch simple concepts in acronyms, scales, scores and fancy names. The Glasgow coma score is no different. It basically is a scoring system for how scrambled a person's brain is. High score, fourteen, good. Low score, three, bad. A simple one to ten scale makes more sense to me but it is all lingo. Like I said.

"He's not going to protect his airway. We need to intubate him."

"Agree, but check out his film." Dan nods over to a large computer screen that sits on the nearby counter. A chest x-ray glows. I step over to get a better look.

"Damn, that's an impressive pneumothorax. Definitely needs a chest tube."

"Yes ma'am. That's what you're here for."

The body is an exquisitely put together organism in many ways. But it is also quite simple at certain level. It likes things to be in the correct places. Blood in blood vessels, air in lungs. When the blood gets into where it shouldn't be, bad things happen. Same thing

51

with air. In this case, air has escaped out of a hole in the lung, filling the chest cavity and squishing the lung to a useless blob of tissue.

That's where I come in. My job is to put things back where they belong, as much as possible. In this case, getting the air out of the chest cavity to allow the lung to re-expand and go back about its business. Hence the chest tube.

Of course it never fails. As seldom as I wear real clothes, it always seems to end in my being involved in a bloody trauma. At least the patient is not exsanguinating from a gaping wound. That would be blood where it doesn't belong, on the floor. Hopefully I can manage to keep somewhat clean.

"Can I get a gown? Size six and a half gloves."

A nurse pulls a pack out of the cabinet and unwraps it. I quickly slip into the gown as the nurse ties it behind me. I slip on a facemask with a protective plastic eye shield followed by a pair of sterile gloves.

Another nurse has pulled up a tray of instruments to the side of the patient.

"Can you hold his arm up out of the way?"

The nurse grabs the man's wrist and elbow and gently lifts his arm away from his body revealing the side of his thorax.

I beginning feeling from the armpit down, counting the ribs as I go. Finding the space between the fourth and fifth ribs I pause, scalpel hovering just above the skin.

"You're sure he's out? I don't need him bucking when I do this." I look up at Dan who stands at top of the stretcher.

"Yup. Go for it."

I quickly slice through the skin and the underlying fat. It oozes a bloody yellow fluid and falls away under my blade. He's a fat guy so it takes a couple of passes to get down to the ribs. When I can see the ribs, I put down the blade and use my index finger to feel along the upper edge of the rib. Nothing in the way. I take a large curved clamp and grip it firmly in my right hand. Guiding the tip with my left hand, I press it firmly against the tissues above the rib.

There is where medicine turns from finesse to brute strength. I push hard up and in on the grips of the clamp. The tissues hold firm for a moment, and then with a pop, the clamp suddenly slides freely into the lung cavity. A small rush of air confirms the diagnosis. I open the grip, spreading the clamp tips to widen the hole.

Placing my index finger into the hole, I remove the clamp. Sweeping my finger around, I feel for any adhesions, fluid or lung tissue. Satisfied it is pretty wide open, I wiggle around the hole, stretching it a bit more.

The nurse hands me a large diameter plastic tube, about the size of an extra-extra-large straw, with a row of holes along the end inches of the tube. I place the tip of the tube into the hole alongside my finger. Satisfied the tip is in far enough, I slide my finger out and push the tube deeper into the chest cavity.

The overlying soft tissues fall back across the incision site, creating a seal around the tube. I throw a quick stitch with some suture into the skin and wrap it around the tube several times securing the tube in place.

"Go ahead and intubate him, Dan. We need another film too."

The patient hasn't stirred throughout the procedure, which doesn't make me feel good. He hasn't received any medicines to sedate him, so there's a good chance he has a significant head trauma.

I glance at his bloodied face. There are no signs of waking. "Once we have his airway, we need head CT. Then get him upstairs to the ICU."

While Dan is placing the breathing tube, I finish examining the patient to find any other substantial injuries. Probably a broken femur on the left. The expected cuts and abrasions but no other open wounds that would make him unstable for the moment.

"Need a left femur film and probably an orthopedic surgeon."

The guy has a long road ahead of him. His lungs will hopefully recover from the blunt trauma without developing respiratory distress syndrome. I don't feel as hopeful about his brain trauma. The body is resilient but sometimes even a resilient spirit can't save it when the brain is gone.

I slip off the gloves, mask and gown and stuff them in the trash. I step over to the curtain closing off the bay from the rest of the emergency department.

"Dan, I'll go do some admit orders. Can you call ortho?"

"Will do once the films are back. You know they won't do jack shit until they have an x-ray."

I give a wry smile. Working in a hospital system is an exercise in interpersonal skills.

"Kate."

I stick my head back around the curtain, having stepped out, back into the general hustle of the ED.

"Yes?"

"You look nice. I think you should go with that look more often."

I roll my eyes and slip out. I ponder whether that was all in jest, or was there a touch of sincere interest in his tone? We've done this before and it didn't work. Thinking about personal relationships with two different men in one night? I have to get a hold of myself. Focus on work. That is the only safe thing.

Chapter 13

I feel much more relaxed as I change out of the big girl clothes and slip back into scrubs and a t-shirt. A pair of sneakers that I keep on hand in my locker in the operating suites makes my feet much happier. When you wear this all day most days of the year, it is torture to wear real clothes for more than a couple of hours.

It is getting past nine PM. The halls are totally deserted now except for a late stray visitor. There is still a lot of night ahead of me. On nights like this, there is always the dilemma of whether to stay in the hospital, crammed onto a twenty-year-old, thin-as-paper mattress on a rickety old bunk bed in the call room, or try to sneak a few hours of real sleep at home in bed. But inevitably, as soon as my head hits the pillow, the pager goes off and I am back here dealing with the two AM trauma.

My deliberation over this matter is halted as the cell phone on my belt chimes that I have a text message.

"Meet me in the library. M."

"Library? At this hour?" I am puzzled as to why Michele, who is supposed to be upstairs working a double, wants me to come meet her in the medical sciences library. But I learned long ago she usually has a good reason for everything, so I no longer question. Okay, well maybe a little.

A bit annoyed at the delay to my escape, apparently my brain in that instant had decided to go home, I turn left at the next hallway crossroads and head off down the dimly lit hallway. The library, at the far end of the hall, gives off no signs of life.

55

I push open the door, squinting into the dimly lit room. Library shelves line the walls and stand in rows like a line of soldiers at attention. I look around for a light switch and find nothing.

"M? What the hell are we doing down here? M?"

At first, my question is met by silence. But then there is a faint sound of fabric brushing on itself. Weird, I think to myself. I continue my search in each aisle.

Just as I round the last aisle corner, Michele comes into view. She is standing perfectly still and silent. A middle-aged, clean-cut man, closely cropped hair, a deep scar across his chin and steel grey eyes, stands behind her.

"What the hell, Michele?"

Her lip quivers as she locks my gaze with hers.

"I'm sorry, Kate. He made me."

"Made you what? What's going on?"

With that, he pushes Michele forward so forcefully she nearly lands at my feet if not for my reaching out to catch her. In that moment I see the Glock .45 in the man's hand and feel the presence of someone else come up behind me.

I glance over my shoulder to see a short, swarthy-looking, young guy, his arms covered in tattoos, extending from the edge of his short shirtsleeves all the way down to his wrist. His hands look shockingly white in contrast to the dark ink and the black semiautomatic pistol in his hand. Another Glock.

"What is this?" I look back towards the older clean-cut guy. He seems to be the one in charge. At least I hope so, for some reason I can't understand. I try desperately to hold my voice steady, to not let the tremor in my vocal cord betray me. My stomach is rolling into a knot.

"Thank you for coming, Dr. McCullough." His voice is calm and steady, his face completely devoid of emotion.

"You say that like I showed up for a speaking engagement. Judging from the gun in your hand, I assume that is not why I am here. I am a good speaker and all, but all you have to do is call my office."

A slight hint of a smile shows on his face. My stomach relaxes just a bit. Sarcasm helps me focus my energy and stay calm.

"I have heard many good things about you, but no, this is not about your speaking topics."

"Then what?" All the while Michele stands next to me. I haven't let go of her hand. I try to keep myself in between her and Mr. Clean Cut, which doesn't make me feel better as it exposes both of our backsides to the tattooed troll.

"We need your help and did not think you would be willing to help without sufficient encouragement."

"Okay, say I am feeling encouraged. What do you want me to help you with? Beyond my surgical skills, I am pretty much not good at anything, so you will probably be disappointed."

He takes a big stride forward and stands directly in front of me, so close I can see the tiny capillaries in his facial skin. The gun still dangles casually at his side. His face shows no emotion or trace of humanity.

"I think you sell yourself short, Dr. McCullough, but rest assured, we did our homework before selecting you. I am sure you will perform brilliantly." A pause. He slowly and deliberately raises the gun and presses it into Michele's forehead. My heart races as my mouth goes dry. Michele closes her eyes tightly, squeezing out a lone tear. "Because if you do not, this fine lady here will be the one who suffers."

I hold my hands up, willing that I can levitate his arm down. "Okay. Stop okay. This isn't necessary. Just tell me what you need and I will do it."

He lowers his gun. The troll clears his throat and glances out towards the hallway entrance. "Come on man, we gotta go."

Clean Cut shoots a look at the troll then looks me dead in the eyes. "We need you to break Mr. Davis out for us."

"Mr. Davis?" I am momentarily disoriented, having lost all concept of the fact that I have patients upstairs that I am taking care of.

"Yes, the gentleman visiting from the jail."

"What? Break him out? How am I supposed to do that? There is a guard with him twenty-four seven. I don't do violence so you are out of luck." The irony of that statement is lost on him.

"No violence needed. You are going to take Mr. Davis down for a MRI. The guard will have to remove the shackles and step out. You will then escort Mr. Davis out the technician's entrance to the MRI suite and meet us on the lower level of the parking garage."

"That's nuts. There is no way the guard will buy that at ten o'clock at night."

"Kate, we both know tests and things get done all night long in a hospital. I know you will come up with some good explanation for the guard so as not to raise any suspicion. By the time he realizes Mr. Davis has escaped, we will be gone."

"And what about me and Michele? What happens to us?"

"We have no interest in hurting you or Michele. Michele is here simply to ensure your compliance with our request. You do what you are asked, and you both walk away."

I close my eyes and take a deep breath, wishing the whole scene away. But when I open my eyes, he is still standing in front of me, still holding the deadly piece of steel. I am all too familiar with the damage it can do.

I give Michele a hug. "Don't worry girl. I'll take care of you." She squeezes my hands, a volume of communication passing without a word.

I turn to Clean Cut. "Okay. You have to give me a little time to do all this, so don't get too impatient."

"I realize that. That is why I am sending Derek here with you. If asked, you will say he is Mr. Davis's cousin, just got in from out of town and couldn't wait to see him. Derek will keep me updated on your progress. He will also let me know if you do anything to jeopardize the project in which case I will put a bullet in Michele's head and Derek will put one in yours. Are we clear?"

I glare at him for a moment, fury bubbling up inside with an overwhelming impulse to punch him in the face. Abruptly I turn and walk out, deliberately bumping into Derek on the way. I refuse to give up all control even though it's not looking good for me on that front at the moment.

Chapter 14

The hospital is a ghost town after hours. There are no visiting hours as in days past, but not too many people are coming and going after evening has turned into night. The lights are usually turned low at the nurses' stations and the nurses are either busy settling patients in for the night or huddled at their workstations documenting their activities. This is usually my favorite time to be there. I can think and have a moment of peace, which is hard to find in the frenetic bustle of daytime in the hospital. Tonight I am not too thrilled with the solitude.

Clean Cut has taken Michele God knows where. I'm stuck with the troll. We cut up several flights of stairs, but he's clearly in good shape and never breaks stride. We come out up the hallway from Davis's room and as expected, there's no one around. But probably for the best as there is no telling what this guy might do if someone stops to talk to us.

I decide to give him a little instruction before we go into the room and have to deal with the guard. I would rather not have a gunshot victim to work on tonight that resulted from my mishandling the situation. Not to mention what could happen to Michele if I fail to get the patient sprung quietly.

"Okay. So you are Cousin Richard. Follow my lead so we don't make the guard nervous. I'll examine Davis first and then tell the guard I need to take him downstairs for an MRI. Is that okay?" I add a little snide tone to the last.

He nods and lifts his shirt to remind me of the gun tucked in his waistband. Like I'd forget.

I knock gently and crack the door open.

"Hello? Mr. Davis? It's Dr. McCullough."

The guard is laid back in a chair watching Sports Center. Not a surprise. Davis is snoozing in the bed. He looks a bit pale to me. The guard stands as I enter. I nod at him.

"Sorry to bother you guys. I just need to check out Mr. Davis's wound. Heard it wasn't looking so good."

The guard takes a step towards the door. The troll is right on my heels.

"No problem. I'll just step out. Don't like looking at that kind of thing. Don't know how you do it."

He looks questioningly at the troll.

I jump in to avoid a problem. "This is the patient's cousin. I ran into him wandering around trying to find his way here. "

The guard slips past him and steps out into the hall. The troll positions himself in the doorway and nods at me to get on with it.

I decide I might as well take a look at the wound while I am here. I am still his doctor after all. And he is about to leave against medical advice. The wound had looked a little inflamed this morning too.

Davis has woken up by this point. No note of recognition passes between him and the troll, but he doesn't seem surprised to see a visitor claiming to be his cousin.

"Hey, Doc."

I haven't disliked the guy. He has always been respectful to me, but at this moment I truly despise him. I briskly pull down the sheet and pull up his gown to expose his abdomen.

"I just need to check your wound. You feeling okay?"

"It's really hurting a lot. "

I indelicately rip off the dressing. He winces with the pain. The wound, in fact, is looking much worse. The edges are an angry flaming red, and there is some pus forming at the upper edge of the incision. Shit. It really is infected.

I shoot a look at the troll who comes over to the bed to see what is going on. I give him credit for a strong stomach, as he doesn't even flinch.

"What's the problem? Let's get him downstairs."

"The problem is this wound is infected."

"It doesn't look that bad. Just give him some antibiotics and let's get out of here."

"Look, you mental midget. You have the gun, but I am still his doctor and I am telling you, if you take him out of here like this, he is going to get sick as shit and die."

The troll takes a big stride to stand right in my face. I straighten to meet his gaze straight on. We both stare for a minute, sizing each other up.

"Doc, I'm not stupid and I certainly ain't falling for this, so pack him up, tell the guard we are going downstairs and let's go. Okay?"

I open my mouth to protest, but he puts a stubby dirty finger to my lips and presses down. My teeth bite into my lip from the pressure, but I don't turn my gaze. After a moment he drops his hand and takes a step back.

"Now let's go. Or I put a bullet into Mr. Guard out there and one in you, and Davis and I still walk out of here."

Clearly, this is not looking good for my team at the moment. I try to tell myself I shouldn't care if some low life convict, who is about to break out of prison while holding me and my best friend at gun point, dies. But I can't. I think it has more to do with the fact that I don't like anything I do to fail and losing a patient, no matter how worthless a person, would just piss me off. But nothing I can do about that at the moment.

Chapter 15

So after tracking down a stretcher and giving an explanation to the guard, we form a little parade through the deserted halls. I am praying not to run into anyone who would be curious about me pushing a patient around to radiology myself. I make the troll take the front end of the stretcher to guide it around corners. That and to keep him away from the guard, who thankfully obliviously traipses along behind us.

I confess I do push the stretcher a bit hard at moments and catch the troll in the Achilles tendon a couple of times. He glares at me but can't do anything more in view of the guard. Now I know I shouldn't be exasperating the man with the gun by doing petty things like that, but I am not good at being sensible, and I am very annoyed at being at his mercy. My poor effort at regaining some sense of control.

I can't say I am relaxing but I am starting to think this preposterous plan might actually work. As long as the guard continues to tag along behind like an unquestioning, obedient puppy. But just when it looks like we are home free coming around the last corner, the threat of disaster approaches in the form of one of the hospital security guards.

The spontaneous impulse to hurl my cookies is instantaneous and overpowering. I stop short, pulling back on the stretcher to stop its forward momentum, scrambling to come up with some innocent sounding, casual greeting.

The troll stops, one hand on the stretcher and one hand on his beltline, his thumb hooked in his pants. It is just a short move from there to the Glock. He stares at me, and cocks his head a bit, and without a word tells me to get rid of the guy or he will.

"Hey Bobby." I force what I am sure is a pitiful smile.

"How ya' doing, Doc?" Bobby continues walking towards us, the large ring of keys jingling on his belt. A Taser hangs next to them. How I wish I could use that thing on the troll.

Bobby comes to a stop midway alongside the stretcher. Glances down at Davis who at this point looks as white as the sheet he lays on. Even this short trip is taking a toll on him. I can't help thinking this breakout is not going to work out well for him.

Time seems to stop moving as we all stand frozen. The troll is now behind Bobby and the prison guard stands behind me. My brain scrambles to figure out if there is some way to alert Bobby to what is going on without tipping off the troll. As the troll is staring intently and viciously at me, there is nothing I can come up with.

Taser versus .45 is pretty poor odds, so there is really no way out of this situation other than to get rid of Bobby without raising suspicion.

I startle a bit at the sound of Bobby's voice. "What ya' doing pushing patients around here in the middle of the night?" I can't tell if Bobby is just making small talk or if he really is wondering what I am doing. It is a question I can't really answer to much satisfaction for someone who knows how the hospital works, but I have no choice but to try to come up with something.

I force another smile, try to look relaxed as my heart pounds like a jack hammer in my chest. "Transport is shorthanded. I really need to get this guy down to MRI so I told them I'd bring him down." I can only pray that it sounds less lame to Bobby then it does in my own head.

Again time freezes as Bobby takes a moment to ponder this. Why can't there be a code atlas at this moment, some rowdy patient or family member making a scene somewhere that requires his immediate attention? I can picture Michele and Clean Cut somewhere, him pacing back and forth looking at his watch, waving his gun around.

Something resembling a prayer passes through my thoughts. I take a deep breath as the troll starts to get a bit restless, shifting his weight back and forth. Fortunately the prison guard seems bored with the whole thing and is just standing by dutifully waiting for the entourage to resume our journey.

Bobby turns to look at the troll who manages to give a creepy insincere smile. To me it only serves to make him look guilty of something, but I hope Bobby buys it. A moment passes before Bobby nods his head in greeting and speaks to the troll. "How are you, sir?"

The troll continues to rock back and forth, looking a little nervous himself but he manages to croak out a reply. "Good. Good. Just worried about my cuz here." He taps Davis on the foot for effect. What follows is one of those awkward moments like occur in an elevator. Everyone sharing a common space, but no one quite sure whether to speak or make eye contact.

In my brain I imagine the distinct whistle that plays in westerns when there is about to be a showdown.

Suddenly the tense silence is invaded by the squawk of Bobby's radio. To me it sounds like fantastically loud fingernails on a blackboard. A phantom voice over the radio speaks "Bobby, need you out at the helipad to secure it for a bird coming in."

Bobby tips his head and squeezes the mic hanging over his shoulder. "On my way."

It is at this point I think I resume breathing, which I believe I had stopped doing after that last deep breath. Another warm smile so as not to screw up at the very last moment when success is within view. "Good to see you, Bobby."

I bend forward over the stretcher, starting it going again. This time I restrain myself from running over the troll, as I am pretty sure something bad would come of it.

Bobby pats me on the shoulder as he starts walking down the hall in the opposite direction that we are going. "You too, Doc. Stay out of trouble."

The very height of irony but I don't feel very amused by it. "Me? Always."

Chapter 16

At this moment I am actually thankful for the prison guard who is still a very real threat to my successfully saving Michele and me. But his presence serves to restrain the troll who looks like he would hit me just for fun. Like I can control who walks down the hallway in a hospital. I am a surgeon, not God.

After one more turn, we make it to the MRI room with no further adventures. Now for the next big hurdle. Turning to the guard, I point at the handcuffs and foot shackles Davis is still wearing, despite looking like he could barely get himself off the stretcher.

"Those have to come off. MRI."

The guard looks at me skeptically, unsure.

"MRI. As in Magnet. Big giant magnet. Which will rip his hands off. Not to mention totally break the machine, which will mean my head. "

"It's against policy to take a prisoner out of shackles. I would have to put some plastic zip ties on him."

"Well, if you have to. But I have to get this done now. We don't have time for you to go getting some from the jail. And really, look at him. What's going to happen?"

The guard hesitates, looks back and forth between Davis and me. I suspect he is thinking about what happened to the poor guard who was in the bathroom allowing the last prisoner to escape.

"I have some in the car."

Troll has made his way over to stand close, next to and behind me. I feel his breath on my neck and the end of his finger as he discretely jabs it in my back. Like I need any encouragement to keep things moving.

"This guy can't wait. He's not going anywhere. He has a raging infection in his gut and I doubt he could even walk, let alone make a break for it. Come on. I gotta get him in there."

The guard ponders all this for another moment, weighing the odds of this scrawny little computer nerd with a stab wound overpowering me and making a break for it. I can barely breathe as time seems to stop. Give me a crashing patient with a gaping chest wound to deal with any day over this stress. My brain keeps chanting "Come on, come on, come on." The image of Michele and Clean Cut once again streaks through my thoughts.

He finally relents and frees Davis who looks quite pleased to finally have freedom of movement after days of shackles. I relax just a bit, which really just means that I am not so wound up that my head is about to explode. I am just left with this churning stomach and the persistent urge to run the troll down with the stretcher and make a run for it. I don't.

"It will take about twenty minutes. You have to stay out here." I push the door open with my butt as I start to pull the stretcher through. "Both of you."

The troll comes up short on this one, not expecting it. But I have to make this believable for the guard. I admit it is also fun to mess with the troll a bit, leaving him twisting. How the hell did he think he could explain being allowed into the MRI room anyway? I am hoping he will not freak out and will take my lead.

"Dick." Nodding towards the troll. "It is Dick right? You had asked about a bathroom before. There is one around that corner to the right and then another right through the double doors."

Now if he is smart enough, he will figure out that I am giving him a back route around to the other exit from the MRI suite and he can meet us over there. A very long moment passes as he tries to read my actions. A light bulb goes on. The mental midget just grew a couple of inches.

The troll grins at me in some ridiculous fashion as if we are two kids on a playground keeping a secret from the teacher. Idiot. "Oh yeah. Thanks."

With that, I pull the stretcher through the door, and it swings closed behind me. Davis doesn't look so good. He is ashen color and grimaces as he sits up on the stretcher. I slide down the railing that keeps patients from rolling off like a three year old learning to sleep in a big bed. He starts to try to stand, but his legs are weak and he buckles back down to the stretcher.

Instinctually, I reach out to steady him. "Whoa, hang on there. How the hell do you think you are going to walk out of here by yourself?"

A flash of anger crosses his face. The most emotion I've seen from him since I first met him. "Look, I had to get stabbed in the damn gut to get this far. I'm leaving here tonight even if I have to crawl to the exit."

It's the first time he has said more than five words to me, and I feel disoriented by the sound of his voice. The whole night's events are so surreal I feel like I am in a bad movie.

I take a step back, unsettled by his hostility. "I'm fairly certain you would but like I told your buddy before, your wound probably is infected. You are not ready for discharge, official or otherwise."

Davis braces his stomach with this arm. All the moving around is clearly hurting him. He glares at me. "You are just saying that so I will be too scared to leave."

"Actually, on second thought, I want you to get the hell out of here so I can get my best friend away from your skanky friend. So no,

I am not trying to scare you into staying. Just full disclosure so I won't feel guilty when they find you dead in an alley somewhere."

Davis' expression is a mix of anger, fear, determination and pain. His eyes narrow down as he looks intently at my face, trying to discern if I am telling the truth or just trying to scare him. Since I am not lying, I don't waiver and I am pretty sure my expression matches my words.

He struggles again to his feet. "I'm leaving." I think about using the stretcher to get him out of the building but why make it easy on him? With several groans and grimaces he manages to hold a standing position just as the back door opens and we are once again graced with the presence of the troll.

"Hi Dick," I say sarcastically. He storms over looking like he is going to hit me but pulls up last minute.

"I should kill you, you damn bitch, but we have to get out of here. Let's go."

Davis takes a few wobbling steps. He's not going to make it much farther on his own. Honestly, I don't know if it is out of a sense of duty to my patient or the knowledge that troll was going to make me help anyway, but I instinctively wrap his arm over my shoulder and grab him around the waist to support him. There was nothing to grab as he is just in the flimsy hospital gown.

"Man, I need some damn pants."

Troll looks at me as if I am the solution to all his problems.

"Doc, can you help us out? Don't you guys have a pile of scrubs around here?"

I glare back for whatever that's worth. "We can stop at the locker room on the way out to the parking garage."

I'm getting more and more anxious to just get out of the hospital and away from any possible showdown with the guard or anyone else we may run into. But at the same time, to be out in the parking garage means to meet back up with Mr. Clean Cut and Michele. They will have what they came for, and Michele and I could be in even bigger trouble at that point.

My head is spinning with thoughts as we limp out the door and down the long empty corridor. No plan seems good. Not that I care if this punk gets away. It isn't worth dying for to keep him in police custody.

No, at this moment, I don't give a damn about Clean Cut, the troll or Davis. They can all go live happily ever after on a damn island for all I care. I just want Michele to not get hurt in any of this. And I have to admit, for all my self-destructive behaviors, I don't want to go down at the hands of some asshole with a gun. But there is no way out other than through the parking garage.

Chapter 17

Thankfully it is a quick uneventful walk, even with a sick, limping patient, from radiology out to the parking garage. As commanded, I grab some scrubs out of the interventional radiology locker room. Good thing, as I end up having to practically drag Davis by his waistband. He's not gonna do well in this. But that's not my concern right now.

The troll leads the way, quite disinterested in providing any help to us. Clearly not a close friend of the man he is breaking out.

"So this was all planned. You were stabbed intentionally?"

Making conversation seems as good a plan as anything. Plus I'm curious.

"Yeah, I was told it was the best way and that I wouldn't get seriously hurt. That was a fucking lie."

"Well that does explain why the wound was low and shallow. Minimal risk of hitting anything of importance."

"Easy for you to say, Doc. All of it feels important to me." With this he gives a little smile. I shake my head in disbelief at the attitude, as if we are just two people chatting. Really?

"You must be important to somebody for them to go to all this trouble."

"You have no idea how dangerous the people I work for are."

"I've had a gun to my head, so actually, yeah, I do have an idea."

The conversation ends as we burst into the lower level of the parking garage. While it feels like eternity, in reality less than ten minutes have elapsed, so we still have a little more time before alarms are sounded. Smart plan choosing the MRI over the CT scan. MRI's take twenty minutes or more while the CT scan is over in minute. Someone with a brain is behind this whole escapade. Hopefully he or she is smart enough not to worsen the situation by including an order to kill a surgeon and a nurse in the hospital garage.

I'm about to find out. The troll beckons me forward. We go past my Jeep, which is about half way down the aisle. There is only a small cluster of cars near the entryway. The evening staff has the luxury of parking nearby in exchange for working while the rest of the world is sleeping. At the far end of the aisle, in the darkest corner, is a nondescript silver sedan, out of which now pops Mr. Clean Cut. He walks around to the passenger side, opens the door out and pulls Michele out by her arm. He discretely holds his Glock in his right hand.

My heart leaps at the sight of Michele. I have not had a fully formed conscious thought that he would actually hurt her before I got there, but apparently my heart has been worried about that. She is rattled but unharmed and just a little bit pissed judging by the look on her face. It is a look only someone who knows her would read as such.

Our entourage comes to a stop next to the car. Davis is looking really puny - pale and sweaty, and clearly is in some significant pain.

"What's wrong with him?" Clean Cut gestures at Davis but looks at me.

"His wound is infected. He needs to stay in the hospital."

Clean Cut cracks a slight smile. The first human emotion I've seen. I don't know whether this is a good or a bad sign.

"Well you are the doctor. Give him some antibiotics and he'll be fine."

"It doesn't work that way. He needs IV antibiotics. Beside, where would you like me to get these antibiotics from? We're in a fucking parking garage." I could feel the heat of anger and fear rising in my face. I have been trying, not entirely successfully, to be an obedient prisoner, but my fear and frustration is starting to get the better of me. Sarcastically I add, "Better yet, I'll write you a prescription and you can stop at Walgreen's on your way out to get it filled."

The smile disappears from Clean Cut's face. I have pushed it too far, as I usually do. I can't help it. He repositions his hand on the gun.

"You better just hope your handiwork was good enough and that he'll be okay, Dr. McCullough."

Now I've done it. Pissed him off just when I need him to be feeling amicable to Michele and me. My mind starts racing, looking for a way to backpedal from the sarcasm.

"I'm sorry. I'm a bit wound up. Just keep clean dressings on it and his body will probably be able to fight it off. He's young and healthy." Now I have no expectation of that being the case, but it seems to be what everyone wants to hear.

"Very good. Now there is one more thing, Doctor."

Oh God, here it is. The moment when the bad guys decide just for the hell of it to try out their shiny new guns and leave the two of us bleeding out on the filthy, oil-stained, gum-laden concrete. I've always thought I would die young, but I never saw it going down quite like this. I draw a big breath in and close my eyes.

"I need your car keys."

My eyes fly open and stare at him, totally taken aback by this last sentence.

"What?"

"Your car keys. Please."

Now fortunately, I had been on my way out of the hospital when all this started so my keys are jangling around in my back pocket. We would be stone cold out of luck if they were in my locker as usual. The fates looking out for me, perhaps?

I pull the keys out and hold them up. The troll, who has been angrily staring at me this whole time, mentally willing daggers into my head with his eyes, snatches them roughly from my hand.

"You're taking my car?" I'm disbelieving and truly pissed. It's the last straw. "Isn't it enough you held a gun to my best friend's head, made me break a patient out who is sick, and now you are going to steal my car? Wait, don't tell me, let me guess. You are planning on torching it in the end to destroy any evidence."

Mr. Clean Cut actually laughs. It rings hollow and unearthly in the caverns of the garage. I am not reassured. I feel like I am skiing full speed down a double black diamond slope with an avalanche closing in from behind. Helpless and just about out of time.

"No, we are borrowing it. You'll get it back in a couple of days once the police track it down. There won't be any evidence left in it."

I want to argue. I want to scream at him and smack his smug face. My brain is screaming inside my skull to do it. But my mind stays firmly in control. I step over to position myself between the trio of badness and Michele.

"You have everything you want. Now just go. We won't say anything about you to the police. Not what you look like, not what you're wearing, not which way you go. I don't give a damn to see you or hear you ever again. So just go."

"I doubt that very much, Kate. May I call you Kate? You'll talk to the police but it won't matter. They won't find us. But we, I, very much appreciate your assistance."

With that he turns and waves his faithful duo to follow him back up the aisle to my Jeep.

"No, you may not call me Kate." I can't help it. The brain wins on that one. It's out of mouth before I know it.

Clean Cut keeps going but at this troll turns around and jogs the few steps back to where Michele and I still stand motionless, watching them go.

"What? You got what you want."

Troll stops toe-to-toe with me. Once again I am graced with his nicotine-infested breath in my face. He holds my gaze in his. I do not look away. An eternal moment passes when I do not take a breath do not blink.

Suddenly, he steps back, cocks his arm back and catches me square in the mouth. A spray of blood burst forth from my lip as my head flies back, my knees give way and I crumple to the ground. I try to keep my eyes focused on the face of the troll, who now appears as double.

"That's for calling me Dick, you little bitch. I'd do a lot more but the boss said not to hurt you. Much."

And with that he's gone and it's over. For the moment.

Chapter 18

If ever there was a moment I wanted to have a drink it's this one. The evil trio has made their exit. The guard has finally figured out we are not coming back out of the MRI room and has sounded the alarm. The hospital, especially the garage, is swarming with hospital security and local and state police.

Someone has rolled a wheelchair out for me. I keep refusing to let them take me into the emergency department. My head is spinning and my jaw is aching. I should go to the ED. It is the wise thing to do and everybody keeps telling me that. Finally I give in just to shut them up. Everything checks out and except for a big fat lip and bruise I am fine, physically at least.

I am, however, getting a bit tired of being someone's punching bag. I have to work on my interpersonal skills. Or at least learn to rein in my tongue. After being examined, I make my way back to the garage to give my statement.

Michele and I are standing off to the side of the chaos, leaning on one of the security vehicles, both lost in our own private interior place trying to restore some semblance of normalcy. The sound of a familiar voice cuts into my retreat. I look up, stunned and speechless as Mike strides up to us. "Hi ladies."

Despite the bland greeting, the electricity in the air is noticeable. Including to Michele.

"Mike...I.." That's all I can get out before my speech fails.

Michele looks inquisitively at me and then at Mike. Mike holds a hand out to her.

"Mike Morgan. Sheriff's investigator. Sorry to meet you under these circumstances."

I still sit dumbfounded, exhausted and disoriented from the night's events.

Michele shakes Mike's hand earnestly, while still looking at me from the corner of her eye.

"Michele Barrett. Can't say I am happy to meet you. Maybe in a nice restaurant or a theater somewhere, but not here."

"I understand, ma'am. I just need to get some information from both of you about what happened."

He looks over at me, studying me. I am lost in the juxtaposition of my date standing in front of me after I was just held at gunpoint and then flattened with a punch. It's all so surreal. All my bravado has abandoned me for the moment.

I look up as he puts his hand on my shoulder.

"Hey, you okay?"

There it is again. That tender tone, that penetrating stare. What is it about this guy?

I clear my throat, regain a sense of composure. I am a trauma surgeon for God's sake. I'm supposed to keep it together.

"Yeah. Yeah. I'm good." I stand up straight, leaving the support of the vehicle that has been holding me up just to prove the point. I hope he doesn't see my legs buckle a little as a wave of nausea washes over me. Okay, maybe I am not entirely fine.

"What are you doing here, Mike? We were just on a date, right? This is all so bizarre. Were you on call too?" In this moment I do not appreciate the irony of this possibility. He does and gives a little grin.

"No. No. But when you left, I figured I had no plans for the rest of the evening so I called the guy who was on and offered to cover. He's got a wife and two little kids at home. Call sucks for him. Didn't really expect to see you again."

I smile weakly. "Well I guess that is the one good thing that came out of all this hell."

He smiles as our eyes lock for just the briefest of moments. But it's long enough for Michele to take it all in and cock her head and roll her eyes. That is her way of saying she is happy for me.

So we spend the next however many minutes going over everything that happened in excruciating detail. Mike takes a bunch of notes and sends a uniformed guy to put out a bulletin on my stolen Jeep.

It is well past midnight. Mike offers to have a uniformed officer drive Michele home. She takes a pass and says she is driving herself home but agrees to let an officer follow her. She has a stubborn streak as long as mine but hides it better. Well, okay not quite as long as mine.

Of course in her post trauma stress and her overwhelming desire to be at home safe with her kids and her husband, she forgets that I am now stranded.

I stand sheepishly in front of Mike. Most of the uniformed guys have cleared out by now.

"Uh, I guess I'm going to need a ride. Can one of your guys take me?"

"Hell no."

"What?" My brain is so tired and drained I am having trouble keeping up with sarcasm.

"I'm driving you myself."

"Oh, okay." I'm too exhausted to come up with reasons why that is a bad idea. In my better moments, there would have been a long list. But not tonight. Boy, do I want a drink.

Chapter 19

The house is dark and silent as the door swings open. Mike goes in first, gun drawn. Half way home I realized my house keys were on the keychain with the car keys and I suddenly felt even more vulnerable. The spare was under the fake rock in the little planting bed outside the front door. Cliché I know, but if I were too clever with a hiding place, undoubtedly I would forget where it was when I needed it. As it is, we have to turn over several rocks until I find the right one. I think Mike finds it amusing although in the dim light of the waning crescent moon, it is hard to read his expression.

Thankfully, on entering, we are met only by Tasha, my cat. I was always a dog person, not a cat person growing up. But my schedule makes it impossible to keep a dog responsibly. The cat happened into my life when she showed up several nights in a row in the hospital parking lot, looking emaciated and ill. I saved it. Big surprise there. She meows several times, apparently put out by the empty food bowl that I had forgotten to fill on my way out earlier. That feels like it was days ago.

Mike checks all the rooms of my two bedroom, two story townhouse. Modest digs for a surgeon, but I am never here so it works well for me. It is cozy, furnished with comfortable practical items. The kind of furniture that can be used rather than shown as museum pieces. A few mementos and pictures but not a lot of knick-knacks. Simple and utilitarian is the way I need things. My living accommodations are probably one of the few simple things in my life. I don't need the ultra large house, or the picket fence or the big back

81

yard with a pool. That sort of thing is for families and that's not me. It's better this way.

I head to the small kitchen, turning on every light I have, as Mike finishes his sweep upstairs. My bedroom and a small guestroom make up the second story. I briefly wonder if I left underwear lying on the bed but it's too late now. Without a word he then pops down to the unfinished basement where my work out equipment is, complete with heavy bag. I don't use it a lot and certainly have no particular skills with it. But it is a good stress reliever after a bad day. I might need to get down there tomorrow.

If someone is here to overpower him we will both be goners as I am exhausted. I really want a drink right now. But I fill up the electric kettle and click it on, deciding to settle for chamomile tea instead. Somehow I don't think it will have the same effect. That is probably a good thing although I am not entirely convinced of it at this moment. The silence is crushing. Flipping on the Bose player, I scroll through my Ipod, settling on Dave Matthews off my play lists. As close to relaxation music as I have. Maybe I need to expand my tastes, try something new.

I plop down on the couch as Mike comes back upstairs. He checks the French doors that lead out back to a little patio area. The dark, still silence of the backyard seems more menacing than I remember it. But the door is locked and secure. He twists the plastic wand that turns the vertical blinds closed.

"It's all clear. You need to get your locks changed first thing in the morning."

"Yeah, I'll call someone. Do you want some tea? That's about all I have other than water." I am slightly proud of the fact that I maintain enough presence of mind to be a polite hostess.

"Nah, I'm good. Is there someone who can stay with you? A friend, family?"

"Not really."

Mike has returned to the living room, curiously taking in all the details like only a cop can do. He picks up a picture of Bode and I play wrestling on the beach, laughing, enjoying life. Our last vacation together. A day that seems like a lifetime ago. "What about this big guy?"

I shrug. "Definitely not him."

Mike's curiosity is clearly peeked. Sizing up the competition? I let him twist for a minute but decide to not play games.

I make my way into the living room and plop down on the overstuffed ultra-comfortable leather sofa. "That's my brother, Bode. He can't be here because he is in prison."

The words are out before I realize I am saying it. It is information I tend not to share. It is either a conversation ender or makes people jump to all kinds of wrong conclusions that just make me angry. But for some reason, Mike seems to disarm me by just his presence. Or it is the after effects of trauma?

"May I ask for what?"

"DUI manslaughter. It was not his fault but he's paying the price."

I don't offer any more and Mike doesn't push for it. I appreciate him all the more for it.

"Well okay then, do you want me to spend the night?"

I take a long hard look at him and burst out laughing. "That is both the fastest move ever and the worst cliché."

Mike grins, then blushes, realizing how it sounded. He has a nice smile, his eyes sparkle and his face lights up with its genuineness.

"I'm sorry. I didn't mean it like that." He sits down on the couch next to me, comfortably closer than I would normally prefer from someone. "But of course if you're offering."

I laugh harder. An almost uncontrollable giggle. Exhaustion and fear mixing in a huge release of emotion.

Mike can't help but start laughing too. "God, I'm not sure how to take this. Hysterical laughter is not usually the response I get."

I finally get a hold of myself, a little giggle bursting through now and again. "No, no. I'm sorry. It's just…" No need to finish that sentence. The emotion is apparent. "That's really sweet of you to offer to stay, but I'll be fine. Really. I am sure those guys are long gone."

Mike grows serious, sitting straighter on the couch, his cop kicking in. "I've been thinking about everything you described. I'm not convinced it was random. After all, you said you and Michele are best friends. How did they know to use her as leverage?"

I sit up too, the uneasiness returning at Mike's suggestion. I put down my cup of tea on the coffee table strewn with medical journals and three-month-old magazines. I buy them with every intention to read them. Just never seem to get around to it.

I fold my hands, rub them together anxiously. I am certainly not portraying the in control surgeon I pretend to be. "I don't know. It does seem like they knew something about me. And they had the whole thing really planned out."

"In what way?"

"Well, they were the ones who wanted me to take him to MRI. Normally for that kind of thing I would CT him. It's a much more common test, so they easily could have asked for that."

"Does it matter?"

"At first I thought it was just so the guard would take off the shackles. A CT wouldn't matter. But the time also worked to their advantage. A CT takes a couple of minutes, an MRI takes twenty minutes or more. The guard wasn't going to become suspicious until we were out of the building."

"I guess that is something they could learn easily enough, off the Internet or something. My question is why did they pick you to help them get away? Was it just coincidence?"

"I'm sure that's all it was. Right person, wrong time. They probably found out I was his surgeon and did a little digging around. Everyone at the hospital knows Michele and I are tight, so they could have picked that up just hanging around. I'm sure it was just that."

I suddenly get a chill. I say I am sure, but with Mike's suspicion shared, the seed of doubt is now firmly planted in my brain. Leaning forward I put my head in my hands, rubbing the back of my head where a nagging ache is building.

I stiffen at the feel of Mike's hand rubbing my back. Instinctive reflex. I take a deep breath and will myself to relax and enjoy the intimacy. I tip my head to look up at him. He pulls his hand away.

"No, it's okay. Feels nice. I'm tired of people hitting me."

"This happens often?" He puts his hand back.

I give a weak smile. "You have no idea. I'm a trouble magnet."

"I like trouble."

The electricity in the banter is palpable. What am I doing? I don't let people in, certainly not a cop. A long heavy moment of silence passes. I want desperately to curl up in his arms and let him make me feel safe, to be my salvation. But there is no salvation for me, and there is no safe place other than alone. Tonight just confirms my belief that anyone close to me just seems to end up bad off.

I stand up to break the spell. A big cleansing breath to regain my strength. "I'm beat. Literally. I'll be okay. You can take off."

Mike stands up beside me. He stands tall at over six feet, towering over me. Works out. Takes care of himself. That is obvious. Stop, I have to tell myself.

"Are you sure?" His face is full of earnestness.

My stomach flutters, this time in a good way but I stand firm in my resolve. "No, no. Really, I'm fine. Just gonna crash in bed."

Mike doesn't look entirely convinced but takes it at face value. "Okay then. Here's my card. It has my office number, cell and email."

He slips it into my bag sitting on the entryway table as he heads towards the door.

"If anything happens, or you need anything. Anything at all, call me. Please."

I trail behind him towards the door to escort him out. He looks apprehensive, tentative. I pat him on the back to reassure him. A warm flush rushes through me. I tend to brush off such blatant display of concern for me, ignore them mostly lest I start to become attached. With him I want to run towards it but a little voice in my head says I will only end up hurting him. Even in the brief time I have known him, I like him too much for that.

"Thanks. I'm sure it's over and I can get on with my life." I say it as much for his benefit as for mine. Truth is, I can't shake this nagging feeling that I'm not entirely done dealing with it.

I hold the door as he steps out into the dim glow of the porch light. He hesitates again. He needs to leave before the stress of the evening breaks down the last of my defenses. I avoid eye contact, looking past him out onto the street."

"You could do one thing for me."

"What's that?"

"Find my damn Jeep. I love that thing."

He laughs. I do too and look up just as he bends down to kiss me. I don't fight. At first I don't respond, but at the touch of his warm lips I give in and return his passion. But only for a moment. I break away.

"You should go."

He clears his voice, takes the first step off the stoop. I close the door as he is still looking back at me.

Leaning against the inside of the door, I close my eyes, exhausted. "I'll be fine as long as you stay away."

Chapter 20

I am nothing if not pigheaded. I refuse to give in despite long odds or ridiculous challenges. It serves me well as a surgeon. It is in this spirit that I decide to go to work this morning. I can't say I slept well. Although surprisingly more than I expected. Sheer exhaustion trumps fear sometimes. Trying not to give it a lot of thought, I go about my routine to get ready for work and on my way. Surely, a few hours of a terror cannot overwhelm the many hours of my life I have spent in the hospital feeling confident and comfortable.

Sometimes I am wrong.

I swing by the police department on my way in to give a description to the police sketch artist. I'm not sure how good my description is even though I can recall their faces in vivid color. The image of Clean Cut keeps nagging me, the feeling that I have seen him somewhere before. The sensation is not that unusual for me. I meet so many people in the course of a day that everyone starts to seem familiar. I decide to attribute this feeling about Clean Cut to that. No doubt he looks like someone I have met at some point along the way through life. Okay, maybe a little doubt. Still no word on my Jeep.

At work, I round on a couple of patients. Nothing all that exciting. A post op bowel resection for a bowel obstruction. Post op ruptured appendectomy. Even though I am a trauma surgeon in a relatively busy mid-sized community hospital, trauma cases alone don't fill all my time. So I have a mix of general surgery patients as well. Gall bladder removals, colon resections, bowel obstructions, appendectomies – it is the bread and butter of a general surgeon.

After recounting the events of the night before for a countless number of times, I find myself increasingly edgy and irritable. I don't know if it is from being asked over and over again about it or having to relive it over and over in the telling. With each retelling, I make it shorter and vaguer. But somehow, as I am speaking, the images in my head grower sharper and more detailed every time.

I need a distraction. I seek it in the Emergency Department. It is good to have friends all over the hospital. I can go hang out down in the ED and if something cool rolls in that is in my field, I get to play too. In this case, it is a minor trauma but involves enough blood and therefore enough adrenaline and attention to distract the endless movie loop in my brain.

Dan is on again today as well and it feels good to stand across the gurney from him. It is as if the fates are pushing us together. A guy fell off a ladder and went through a plate glass window on the way down. No life threatening lacerations but several large ones that are bleeding like stink. So Dan appreciates my taking one leg while he picks out glass and sutures the lacs on the other.

"Thanks for letting me play, Dan."

"Are you kidding? Thanks for the hand. This would take me forever by myself. But it you prefer something more interesting, I have a chick who swallowed a toothbrush in the next bay."

The patient is pretty groggy from the morphine he received so it is easy to forget there is someone under the drape who can hear us chatting. Someone who would likely be horrified to hear our conversations. The same thing happens in the operating room. Any job, no matter how unusual becomes normal to those who do it long enough.

"A toothbrush?" I want to gag just thinking about it.

"She's in jail. Guess she wanted to get out for a while. It's stuck. Couldn't make the turn from the esophagus to the stomach. Said she tripped, knocked it in accidently"

"Yeh, right. Maybe she is practicing to be a sword swallower. People never cease to amaze me. And not in a good way. That had to hurt on the way down though. And no fun to retrieve so I think I'll stay here. Plus I have had my fill of prisoners for a while."

"I bet. I'd ask if you want to talk about it but I'm thinking that is all you have been doing today."

"Got that right."

We both look up as a nurse pops her head through the curtain.

"Doctor Mahoney, we need you in one. CPR rolling in."

Dan looks up at me as he throws a knot in the end of the suture closing up the laceration he is working on. "You good?"

I motion him away. "Go, go. I got this."

"I'll be back."

Dan pulls off his gloves and slips off the paper gown he was wearing and slips out with the nurse.

"Don't bet on it. I'll be done," I call out after him.

Now I am not entirely alone. A rookie nurse is standing by, watching. Ready to assist if needed. But apparently she is either mute, extremely shy or intimidated as she doesn't say much. On a good day, I would try to make her feel more comfortable, make some small talk. It is not a good day.

I wish it were. Silence creates a cavernous space in my brain for the memories of the night before to come flooding back. And like some cruel joke, my brain takes this as an opportunity to bring back other of my worst memories. It is like the neurons charged with remembering life's traumas suddenly all spark to life at once. I jump from one bad memory to the next. And with each, the emotions tied to the events well up like Old Faithful.

My heart rate quickens. I can feel the inside of my gloves getting slimy as my palms start to sweat. The face mask suddenly feels smothering. I try to refocus. Slow my breathing. Focus on the task at hand. Pinch the needle tip with the needle holder. Plunge the steel curve into the skin, looping through the laceration and back up through the skin on the other side. Release the needle and re-grab the tip as it peaks through the skin. Pull it through, the vicryl suture follows behind. Let go of the needle and grab the tail end of the suture now just sticking up above the skin where I started. With my free hand, wrap the suture several times around the needle holder, tightening the loops down around the tail, forming a tight and clean knot against the skin. The edges of the skin come together, ready to begin the healing process.

I repeat this process. And with each suture I place, the control of my mind slips farther away. So much for all those damn relaxation techniques. Some things I guess, you just can't relax through. My goal becomes just to finish the task. One more laceration to go. It's a little one. No big deal. But my heart pounds faster, my chest feels tight, I can't catch my breath, the walls of the room seem to be moving closer. The nurse suddenly speaks and her voice sounds like a cannon in my head. I may actually jump slightly off the floor and I drop the needle holder onto the drape. What did she say?

A hand on my arm. I shudder and pull away.

"Doctor McCullough, are you okay?"

I stare at her. Trying to grasp where I am, what is happening. Every cell in my body is screaming to run, to get away. I have no choice but to oblige. I dig down deep in my brain to regain enough control to attempt to maintain some semblance of sanity and dignity.

"I'm sorry. I gotta go."

I think I mumble something else about just remembering something as I strip the gloves, gown and mask off, shoving them into the trash. Sweat streams down my forehead as I slip out and rush towards the back exit from the ED. It is all I can do not to break out into a full sprint.

I've never abandoned a patient like this before. I have always stayed to the bitter end, no matter how troubling the task. And at this moment, I don't even care. I am sure I will later. But escape is all I can focus on.

It won't always be this way, but for now, the primal brain has won the battle over the rational mind.

Chapter 21

I do not recall the specifics for the moments after that. I need to escape. I need air and sunshine and openness. I probably mutter a few insincere words of greeting to those I pass on my way out. But I suspect the fierce and frightened look on my face make most not even attempt a hello.

I find my way to the open courtyard located near the central part of the hospital, where all the various additions meet. Every hospital I have worked at is the complex patchwork maze of sections added on in countless configurations creating a mind-bending exercise just to get from the front door to your destination. This hospital is no exception. So where there would normally be solid building front to back, there are actually voids. Empty spaces left open to the world. Little patches of the real world that infiltrates the austere, sterile hospital. It is into one of these Garden of Edens that I find myself now.

The warmth of the spring sun and the sounds of life going on outside these walls help me slow down, to focus, to regain control. The tears come spontaneously and uncontrollably for several minutes but the relief that comes with the release of tears also helps somehow. I turn away from the entryway and the glass windows that look out from inside, so as not to be seen in my weakness. A crying trauma surgeon is just not an image most people want to see. Or so I have convinced myself.

The tears finally run out, and I am left in a state of emotional exhaustion. All I feel capable of at the moment is sitting here drinking in the sunshine hoping, like Superman, it can restore my lost strength. I am not sure how long I have been sitting there when the sound of a familiar voice breaks through my isolated world. I look up towards the door to find Dan standing in the doorway.

"May I come in? Or actually I guess it would be may I come out?"

His grin is like a single sunbeam breaking through the dark clouds of a thunderstorm. It makes me think things will be okay. I am not always comfortable with the effect he still has on me, but for now I don't question or push it away. Instead I welcome it as one familiar thing after twenty-four hours of unfamiliarity.

"Out. And yes, you may."

As he approaches, he pauses in front of me. Looks uncertain, unsure how to proceed.

I let him off the hook by patting the bench next to where I sit. "Please sit with me."

It feels so normal, a level of comfort I long for. And with it a conscious unwillingness to consider the wisdom or the truth of it at the moment.

He sits down, leans back on the backrest. Turning his face up into the sun, he lets out a deep sigh. Not a sigh of sadness or weariness or frustration, more like letting out all the stale air in his lungs to let in a fresh full breath of clean outside air.

The instinct to do the same is outbid by the want to look at him. To absorb who he is when he doesn't know I am watching. A moment passes as he sits with his eyes close. Flashes of our time together. Heat and passion. His wanting so much more than I could give him. The awkward days after we broke up but still worked together. It had been nice to pretend that I could meet the love of my life at work, a soul mate to be mine forever like all the couples on those made up medical television shows. But my life is not a fairytale, and I certainly don't expect or deserve happy endings. But despite all this, in my emotionally sodden state I am drawn to him.

He opens his eyes, peeking over towards me. "What? I am just enjoying the fresh air."

I look skeptically at him. "Uh-huh. I'm sure that's what brought you out here, not the fact I had a frigging breakdown in the middle of the ED."

"Well, maybe the nurse did mention you had some issues."

"Issues?" I almost scoff. "That was a nice way for her to put it. I freaked out. I had a damn panic attack in the middle of taking care of a patient. What the hell?"

Dan rests his hand on my leg, it being in continuous bouncing motion from my persistent anxious energy. Just the warmth and strength in his touch is enough to calm me. I look up at him, meet his gaze.

"It's understandable you know. After what happened last night. It's gonna take some time."

"I hate it. I hate it. I hate it. I hate that I lost control last night and even now, I can't get it back. The gun isn't to my head anymore but it might as well be. I still can't slow everything down, focus, forget about it, be in control."

"God Kate, who could? It hasn't even been twenty-four hours. Give yourself a break for once, huh?"

I lean back, wipe away the few remaining tears that cling to my cheeks as if in suspended animation. "I don't do breaks. Breaks are for people who deserve them. Who have earned them."

A moment of silence hangs between us. It occurs to me I revealed more than I wanted in that simple statement. A demon streaked by in my brain and left a trace of evidence of its existence in the words I spoke. But Dan, in his kindness doesn't force the issue.

He just lets the words fall as he wraps his arm around my shoulder and pulls me into himself.

My brain is so exhausted, so overwhelmed by the unfettered emotions of the last day that I allow myself the warmth of him. I take in his smell; I feel the softness of his skin against mine. He is a truly good man. I have never seen him be ugly or cross or impatient or unkind. He is funny as hell and smart as a whip. He deserves so much better than I am, then I can be. I tried to tell him that before. I wanted to keep our relationship light, meaningless, casual, physical. It wasn't enough for him. But I couldn't risk hurting him. I know it would happen if I tried to be more for him. But I couldn't explain why to him either. It left a chasm between us even as we both still care for the other.

I pull away, look over at him. "How did you know where to find me anyway?"

He now takes my hand in his. God how I want more from him at this moment. "Kate, while you are busy saving the world, there are still people around here that really care about you. I know you, remember? As much as you let anyone. I know where you go when you need space."

I look away. The honesty, the vulnerability in his face cuts like a scalpel into my defenses, the walls I have carefully crafted to protect the world, to protect him from my demons. Or maybe it is more to protect myself.

Mercifully, the moment is broken by the ring of my cell phone.

I slip it out of the back pocket of my scrubs. "Hello? Yes this is Kathryn McCullough" I listen to the voice on the other end as Dan looks at me questioningly. "Okay. Yes. Thank you. I will start making arrangements. Thank you for letting me know."

I click the disconnect button, lost in a moment of history. A face I haven't seen, a voice I haven't heard since I was fourteen years old. But my life has been shaped by him every day since in some small way. Suddenly the moment seems surreal, like I am on the stage of life with the cosmos waiting eagerly to see my reaction.

A heavy sigh by me now, one of pure exhaustion. "It is official now. This is one of my worst weeks ever."

"Now what? Who was that?" Dan is all business now, always the doctor ready to tackle a problem, logically and head on.

"A lady upstate. Apparently she manages a retirement community where my Dad was living."

"And… is he okay?"

"No, he's dying"

"God, Kate. I'm so sorry."

Dan was my source of physical comfort for a long time. But beyond that, I never shared myself. We rarely talked about my family. So now an awkward moment exists as he debates whether to inquire.

I let him off the hook. Maybe the panic attack has sapped my energy or maybe I just am tired of hiding. "I haven't seen him since I was fourteen when he walked out on my mom to drown his life in a bottle. But this lady said he asked her to call me. He knew where I was and how she could find me. Has he been keeping track of me all along and I never knew it?"

"I don't even know what to say, Kate."

"Me neither. Certainly not something I was expecting. He wants to see me. He asked the nurse to contact me. What about Bode? God, I wonder if I can get my brother out for it."

To his credit, Dan lets this slip by without question or comment. Getting a family member "out" for a family emergency should prompt questions. It's not normal. But he doesn't push. It didn't use to be this way. He used to press for answers, for explanations. Not anymore. Which makes me want to trust him now more than ever.

"My Dad was an alcoholic. He worked as a stock broker. Did great when I was little. His company went belly up. His partner went to jail. He couldn't land another job. Thought he was black listed. He started drinking. Once he started, he couldn't stop. My mom couldn't take it. One day he just left. Wrote me a note saying how he loved me and was proud of me and that I was better off without him dragging me down. That was the last time I heard from him."

"Kate, I had no idea. I'm so sorry." The sympathy in his eyes is true and genuine. While he was the one who ended our relationship, it is clear that it was more a result of my choices than it was his.

"Not like I ever shared it with you. Maybe I should have. Suffice is to say, my Dad left me quite a legacy when he left. One I seem to have lived down to many times since."

Am I baiting him? Do I want him to ask more questions of me? Do I want to be able to say it all out loud? I am an alcoholic. Someone died at my hand. The fact it was indirectly is only a technicality. I still want to drink every day. I can't bear to have someone care about me, as it will always end badly for them, and for me. I want to feel loved and safe and accepted by someone, by him, but that possibility is just an illusion, a fantastical wish of a childish mind. Do I want to demolish all the carefully constructed walls in one fell swoop, with one brutally honest conversation? Do I want someone to look inside me, to ask the hard questions?

But he doesn't ask. And I don't open the floodgates. And I know it is better this way.

Chapter 22

For reasons I cannot fully identify, I am now sitting in the front seat of Mike's car, headed upstate in a long shot effort to make it in time to see my father. It has all happened without a lot of thought. The decision to agree to my father's wish to see me before he dies. The invitation to Mike to accompany me on the trip. Maybe it was the exhaustion of my brain after the panic attack. Maybe it was all too much, meeting Mike, feeling drawn to him, being held at gun point, having a panic attack in the middle of work, feeling old emotions towards Dan, hearing from my father after so many years. Maybe all the neurons in my brain are rebelling and refuse to follow my usual ways. Instead I am vulnerable and open and terrified. Willing to admit I need a source of comfort and Mike, for some reason, provides that for me at the moment. Maybe tomorrow, I can regain some sense of myself. But for now we travel on.

Mike is kind enough to allow for silence. The invitation was accidental, mostly. He called to check on me, as I was getting ready to leave to see my father. Without thinking, I blurted out what I was doing and surprisingly found myself asking if he wanted to come with me. So here we are.

I finally break out of my merry go round of thoughts. "I really appreciate you driving me Mike."

He glances over, a slight smile curls his lips. "No problem. Glad I called when I did."

Since he had no news on the case, it was clear the phone call had simply been him checking on me. I like the idea. Maybe my luck isn't all bad these days. "Fortuitous, I'd say."

"Want to talk about it?"

"It? There are so many its right now." I say wistfully.

"Dealer's choice. Whatever it you want. Or none at all."

"Well I guess I owe an explanation about my father."

Mike steals another thoughtful glance over at me. The setting sun casts a warm orange glow on his face. It highlights the fine laugh wrinkles around his eyes. "You don't owe me anything Kate. I'm just here if you want to talk."

I sigh heavily. Exhaustion and a sense of safety with this man combined in the exhalation. "There is a lot to it but suffice to say, I haven't seen my father in 18 years. He walked out on us when I was fourteen years old. Never looked back. Or so I thought. "

The emotions surrounding my relationship with my father are complicated to say the least. Anger has long had the lead. And it still would now if I had the energy to be angry. Instead I feel defeated by life, ready to just take whatever it brings. And right now, it was bringing my father back into my life. However brief.

Mike shrugs. "Must be hard to face seeing him now, after all these years. Especially with him so sick."

"It's confusing to say the least. There is so much I've wanted to say to him. To yell at him. To ask him why. And now it all seems pointless."

"But if it gives you some closure, I think you have the right to say whatever you need to."

It was my turn to glance over at Mike. In a different time, I would have pushed him away, run away before I got caught in the web of caring, before I could hurt him or be hurt by him. Like I have done countless times before. But he was different. Or maybe I was different. At the moment, I just felt grateful for him.

"I'm not sure what I will say. I guess it depends on how he is doing. Hell, he might not even be alert enough to have a conversation with me."

"He did ask for you to come, right?"

"Yeh, that's what the nurse said. I don't know. We'll see. Can I ask you something?" I suddenly felt the need to change the conversation to something not about me. Instead, I want to know something more about Mike. Not casual chatter. No, I need to see something of his soul. Maybe it is because I have bared my own to him. Maybe it is my curiosity and attraction to the glimpse of his inner self that I saw over diner.

"Shoot." He glances over at me.

"Tell me about you and Chase."

Mike lets the question sit for a moment in silence. I don't sense an unwillingness to discuss it, just an effort to assure some composure in sharing it.

"Chase and I were buddies since high school. Not super tight back then. But then we both joined the Marines straight out of school. Two kids thrown into this huge world. So we vowed to always watch each other's backs."

"That's the kind of friends everyone should have." The mental image of Michele flashes through my brain. A warm sense of gratitude to the universe for her.

"We ended up in the same combat platoon in Iraq. Went through hell and back. We both lost some good friends there but we always made sure the other made it out alive. He saved my ass on several occasions."

"I imagine that kind of intensity makes a friendship mean even more than a marriage or something." Not that I had much experience at marriage relationships.

"Yeah. My wife was jealous I think." I can't tell if he was joking or sincere in the comment. I have a fleeting interest in the idea of Mike having a wife but file it away for a later conversation.

"So you both joined the force when you got out of the service?"

"Yup. He wasn't sick to death of me yet so we decided to keep a good thing going. Wish he had gotten tired of me. He'd be alive today if he had."

Of all the emotions in life, guilt is one I have a good handle on so I recognized it quickly in Mike's tone. "I don't know about that Mike. How could it be your fault? Sounds like Chase was doing exactly what he wanted to be doing."

"Yeah. He was. But I can't help but want a different outcome."

"What happened? If you are okay talking about it."

Mike's knuckles turn a little white as he re-grips the steering wheel a bit harder. The stress of memories coming out through his physical actions. "It's okay. I'm learning to make peace with it. We were on the graveyard shift. Still in uniform. Got a call for a domestic disturbance. We both hated those calls. Too many emotions make people unpredictable."

"So true, I have stitched together more than one person involved in domestic violence." It is true. The harm that two people who say they love each other can do to one another is unrivaled in its brutality and cruelty.

"Add the paranoia of a crack dealer who is using his own product and it makes for a lethal situation. That's what happened. We were standing on the front porch. Chase was knocking. We could both hear the screaming inside. I should have pulled him back. I should have gone first. Our knock was answered with a shotgun blast through the door."

Mike's voice cracks with the raw emotions. Certain images just grow more crisp and clear over time, enhancing the exquisite pain that comes with the memories.

"We'd done knock and announces hundreds of times. I don't know why we weren't more careful. Stay out of the line of fire. It would have been so simple."

I instinctively place my hand on his leg, a small attempt to provide comfort. To let him know he is not alone in his anguish. "How could you know Mike? Life is full of assholes. And no matter what you do, sometimes they inflict their evilness on others."

"Still. I should have known better. We were lazy, complacent. After dealing with all those crazy suicidal jihadists in Iraq, perps here seemed pretty tame. Most don't want to die. Most don't want to suffer. But this guy, he wanted to kill someone, no matter what it cost him."

"Where is he now? In jail?"

"Six feet under. He wanted to die. And after what he did to Chase, I was more than happy to oblige him." A flash of intense anger and hatred crosses his face. The things we are capable of when pushed to the brink of fear and pain.

"He left me no choice. Was holding his wife at gunpoint. Then he turned his gun on me so I put him down."

"What happened to Chase?"

"It all happened so fast. He took a blast to the chest. I shot the perp and then I held Chase in my arms as he took his last breaths. So fucking Hollywood cliché I know, but it's what happened. Got out of uniform right after that. Couldn't walk around the streets with a bulls-eye on my chest anymore."

103

It's hard to know what to say after a story of such gravity. Like telling someone their loved one is dead. You can want to comfort, but are there really any words that do that? So I go with the simple, but true. "I'm so sorry Mike."

His hand finds its way to mine, where it still rests on his thigh. He squeezes it. Exhales deeply, as if releasing all the emotions out of his body. "Thanks Kate. I'm really glad I'm here with you."

I look over at him as he glances at me for a brief second. "I'm glad too."

Silence settled in the car but again it is the comfortable silence that exists between two people who are so familiar to each other that the spoken word isn't needed. How this could exist between us now, having just met, is a mystery to me. Another mystery of the mind. But however it could exist, I was thankful for it as it makes the passing moments easier.

Chapter 23.

I spend most of my life in a hospital so the setting should feel familiar. As I walk down the hallways in Moorehead Memorial Hospital, in some ways, it does. But in another way, I feel like I am sleep walking. Traipsing through a dream world that is not my own. Mike is waiting down in the lobby.

Passing by the nursing station on the cardiac wing, I give a nod of hello to the nurses sitting at the desk. The sign on the wall indicates my father's room is just down the next hallway. I pause at the entrance to his room. The door is shut. Butterflies fly wildly around in my stomach. Is it nervousness? Fear? Anger? All of the above?

I take a deep breath and knock quietly, pushing the door inwards at the same time, listening for a reply.

Then I hear it. "Come in." Weaker, frailer, thinner than I remember but it is still the deep baritone that has played in my memory for years. His laugh. His soothing tone when I was hurt. His cheering the loudest when I scored a goal playing soccer. A flood of memories, all jumbled together flash through my mind.

I stick my head around the door, say a quiet and tentative "Hello?"

He looks lost in a sea of white sheets. His six foot frame filling the length of the bed, but his muscular frame has wasted away to just a thin ghost. His hair is silver grey. His cheeks are sunken in. His color ashen. His breathing is fast and heavy. The whistle of the

105

oxygen blowing though the tubing in his nose penetrates the quiet of the room.

For a moment, I stand, unseen by him. But then he turns his head from where he had been staring out of the window into the early evening dusk. His sapphire blue eyes shine as his face lights up with the smile that comes up instantly. I am not sure why, but despite my anger and pain, his smile is matched by mine. But they are both tinged with sadness.

"Oh Kate." That is all he can manage before a cough interrupts. End stage heart failure demands all one's oxygen go to vital functions. There is little left for conversation.

"Hi Dad." I want to be angry. I want to yell at him. I want to tell him how much I hate him. But for the moment, all I see is a frail dying man. One that I loved at one time. One who was my whole world once in the past.

I pull up a chair next to his bed and sit down. He reaches out his hand to hold mine. I oblige. His feels cool, fragile. Existing in the vestibule of death. He squeezes mine as a tear gathers in the corner of his eye. "I am so glad you came. I just wanted to see you, to see you face one more time."

I can feel tears well up in my eyes, a lump in my throat. What emotions are behind it I do not know. I can't gather a complete sentence to speak. So we just sit for a moment, holding hands. Connecting again after years of isolation.

I finally compose myself. The shock of seeing him wearing off. The reality that is our relationship returning. "It is good to see you too Dad. I'm sorry that you are sick. But why? Why does it matter? Why do I matter now, after all this time?" I can't or maybe don't want to mask the bitterness in my voice.

"Oh Kate. You don't know. You can't know. There is so much I wish I could explain."

"There is no explanation. None that matters anymore, Dad. It's too late. I understand why you would want to see me now. To make atonement. To ask forgiveness. I wish I could grant you that. I really do. But it's not me. It's not there."

I should be kinder. I should lie to him. Comfort him in his dying hours. But I can't. I can't erase all the years that I hated him, felt hurt and abandoned. I had stopped imagining a reunion years ago. So this moment, sitting here in a hospital talking to a man who, while sharing my genes, is a stranger to my life.

He turns his head to look out the window again, wipes a tear with his free hand. "I know how angry you must be Kate. I can't change that."

He turns back to look at me. Reaches to pat my hand which he still clings to, with his free hand. It takes tremendous effort. He rests for a moment, catching his breath. "Tell me about your life Kate. Are you happy? Do you have someone special? I don't want you to be alone."

It is my turn to look out of the window. I think through all the events of the last couple of days, of Mike, of Bode, of all the wreckage that lays strewn on the shoulders of my life's path. And then I lie. "It's good. I'm happy. I love my work. Good friends. It's all good."

I can't give him any more details. He has no right to be proud of any good I have may have accomplished and I don't want his pity for all the failures and emptiness that exist for me. But it turns out he is more informed than I think.

"A trauma surgeon. I always knew you would be a doctor. All those years trying to patch up the injured bird or dying squirrel or whatever creature you found in need." We both smile weakly, thinking about the dozens of stray or abandoned, some injured, some just afraid, that I brought home to save. How naïve is a child, to believe she can really save a life, change a life. But then again, isn't that what I spend my day doing still? And sometimes I succeed. Idealism dies hard.

"Obviously you have been keeping track of me to some degree." As much as I want to be angry, I am touched by this fact.

"I may not have been there every day for you Kate, but I've always kept an eye on you and your brother." The mention of Bode brings a guilty lump to my throat. And apparently a look on my face that my father can read. "He'll be fine Kate. He's a survivor. He'll be out soon and can go back to building a great life. You shouldn't worry about him."

I should ask how he knows all of this, inquire about what details he knows and is not sharing. But the confusing thoughts racing around my brain make it difficult to pursue a single line of questioning. Instead, I fall back on the anger that has been my small comfort for years.

"I don't get it. You obviously have been somewhere in the shadows of our lives. Why not just show yourself? Why not man up and be a real father? And why, now, after all of these years, do you show yourself. Call me? What's the point?"

He closes his eyes, purses his lips as his breath grows thin and more labored for a moment. A grimace of discomfort. "There is too much to explain. And no time. Only a heart transplant can save me now. And it's a long list. So I just needed to see you once before I die. To tell you something."

"There it is. It's always been about what you need. Not what I need. So why should I wonder it is no different now?"

He looks back at me, my eyes ablaze with anger and resentment. "I deserve that. I deserve everything that you are feeling towards me. I didn't ask you to come to seek your forgiveness. I know that is too much to ask."

"Then why dad? Why am I here? Why couldn't you just leave everything in the past where I have learned to leave it?" I slip my hand out of his, rub my face with my hands and lean back, arms crossed, closing myself off from caring, from losing him all over again.

"To warn you."

"Warn me?" A snorting laugh almost escapes me. "Warn me about what? That my dad is an asshole. That my father is a coward who abandoned his family and I should have nothing to do with him? News for you. I learned that a long time ago."

I know I am being incredibly harsh on a man who his on his deathbed. I should be kinder. More understanding. More forgiving. But I can't find it in me at the moment. Instead, the idea of him watching me from the shadows, seeing but not wanting to be a part of my life, serves to fuel my anger and pain. It outweighs all the quieter conflicting emotions. To his credit, he doesn't flinch. He doesn't turn away from my fury, by bitterness. "No Kate, I get that. I just want you to be careful."

"Careful?" I barely stifle another shrill laugh. "That's richly vague. What the hell does that mean?"

He tries to scoot himself up in the bed a bit. It takes tremendous effort and all of his breath. I watch quietly, waiting for him to recover from the effort. He pants heavily for a moment, an audible wheeze whistles from his lungs. He doesn't have long left in this world. Oddly, despite my growing frustration and hostility, I find the thought that I am glad I made it in time to see him streak through my brain.

"I made choices Kate. Ones that put everyone I loved at risk. I tried to protect you. But I made a mistake. I was sick. I didn't want to be alone. I am so sorry."

"What the hell are you talking about?"

"It's too late Kate. I won't last but a few more days. I hope that will bring an end to all of it. But I just wanted you to be aware. To always watch out for yourself."

"I've been doing that for a long time now Dad. So don't worry on that count."

Another coughing spell interrupts. I suspect he is right about it only being days. His heart has given out and no amount of medicine was going to fix it at this point. The coughing wears him out. His wheezing grows louder. Much as I want to force the issue, to finish saying all the things I want to say, to hear and dismiss all of his explanations and rationalizations, I know that it is not possible. This man who was my father for 14 years before he was a ghost for eighteen is dying in front of me. As angry as I am, I can't steal precious minutes from him and I can't let his last moments be smothered in anger and hatred. The damage is done. What good comes from more anger?

"I'm going to go dad. You need to rest." I grab his hand again. It is ice cold as he squeezes mine.

"Just sit with me a little bit Kate?" He is tentative, wishing more than asking.

I relax back into the chair in which I had by now perched myself on the edge of, ready to bolt from the room. Much as I want to run away, I can't be so cruel to a man who is dying. Not to a man who was, is, after all still my father. Maybe it is out of respect for that simple fact. Maybe it is out of gratitude for the fourteen years he was a part of my life. Maybe it is out of simple kindness to a stranger who seems to have no one else. So I stay.

He drifts off to a fitful sleep. The gurgling and wheezing of his breath creating an unsettling symphony of noise in the room. My mind dances around the rooms of my life, my past, my present and my future. My mother and how she strived to raise us by herself. The

110

accident. My descent into the bottle. The destruction of the best relationships I've had. The sense of helplessness at the gun aimed at Michele and me. The unsettling but welcome sense of safety I feel with Mike. Mike. The poor guy is sitting downstairs in the lobby patiently waiting for me.

We just met. We barely know each other. But like déjà vu or some sense of existing together in another life, I feel inexplicably drawn to him. I can hardly admit that I now find myself wishing, hoping for something real, something meaningful with him. Is it the pain in his eyes when he talks about the loss of his partner? Is it the sense of security I feel when he is around? Is it simply just physical animal attraction? Is it just because I am worn down and vulnerable from the events of the last couple of days? Is it my imagining it as something more than it really is? I have no idea. But I find myself wishing for it more than anything else I can think of.

I am not sure how much time has passed when my father finally stirs again. The dusk has given way to the full darkness of night. A tiny sliver of moon is all that illuminates the night sky. The dim yellow fluorescent light over the head of the bed casts shadows in the room.

He smiles weakly as he sees I am still here. I return his smile with my own. His voice is barely a whisper. "Hey."

"Hey yourself. It's late. I am going to go so you can get some more rest."

He reaches out to hold my hand once again. It's ice cold in my own.

"Just promise me something Kate."

"What's that Dad?" It feels weird to say that word out loud after so many years of not having someone to address as that.

"Just be careful Kate. There are bad people in life. Some who never forget, even what is ancient history."

I stand up, still holding his hand. Bending over, I kiss him gently on the cheek. I vaguely think to ask what exactly he is talking about. But he seems so frail that I am afraid to press any conversation. So I simply accept it as the worries of a dying father for his daughter.

"Okay, I'll be careful. I promise. Now please get some rest. We can talk tomorrow."

A smile crosses his face, wistful, full of regret but touched with relief, with a sense of release. "I know I hurt you Kate. But please know, I always loved you. Always."

Our eyes meet and hold for a moment. I search them for the truth in his words. And I find it there. For whatever it is worth.

"It's okay Dad. Really. Please just rest."

I head towards the door. As I swing it open to leave, I turn back, looking at the ghostly figure left behind. "Take care of yourself Dad. I'll come back. Okay?"

He smiles again. "Okay Kate."

I swing the door shut. As I lean up against it for a moment, a tear makes its way down my cheek. I feel like an emotional dishrag, ready to crumble to the floor. "I love you too Dad." It is barely a whisper but I say the words out loud that I've denied to myself for so many years. I want more now. I want to have more time with him.

But somehow, we both know that it is the last time we will see each other. The phone call comes before I even make it all the way home.

Chapter 24

I had expected to sleep like a hibernating bear, the mixture of
emotional and physical exhaustion creating a void of thought that
would open to a deep and peaceful sleep. It doesn't work out quite
that well for me. Instead, I awaken from a restless, troubled sleep.
During the night, I felt more like a chicken on a rotisserie, spinning
around endlessly, looking for a position of comfort and release.

As the first orange streak of sunshine knifes across my
bedroom, I give it up and climb out of bed. I pad downstairs into the
kitchen for coffee. God bless the person who invented the Krups
coffee cup machine. Quick and perfect every time, no measuring, no
little pile of coffee grounds on the counter where I missed on the pour
into the machine.

I consider the day ahead. Judging by the shaking in my hand
as I lift the coffee cup to my lips, it is probably best I am not going to
operate today. The last thing a wounded, traumatized person needs is
a surgeon with a tremor. Between the violence and then the fear,
highlighted by my panic attack, it is clear I need some time away
from work. It pisses me off that it has affected me so much.

I have worked hard at crafting a cool, calm, detached,
levelheaded persona. When the world around me is getting ever more
chaotic and people are panicking, I only grow calmer and more
focused. That's how it works in the hospital when people are trying to

die. Apparently from my brain's point of view, having a gun shoved in my face is a totally different animal.

I refuse to surrender completely, but I do compromise with a strategic retreat from the place that is haunting me, the hospital. I need to get away from the events, go do something completely different and separate. What exactly is the big unknown. I work, I sleep. That is my life for the most part. I really do need to get a hobby. I settle for going for a run.

I hate running. It strikes me as something that should really only be done when someone mean and ugly, or something big with sharp teeth is chasing you. But it is a good way to burn off discordant, uneasy restless energy. And since I usually have a lot of that, I run. At least it is better than standing on a stair stepper or elliptical machine sweating your butt off and getting absolutely nowhere.

At the two mile mark, I call it quits and turn for home. Four miles total. And by the end, I am almost relaxed enough to stop startling at every approaching car, slamming door, or loud noise.

After a quick shower, I go to work on the phone making arrangements for my father's funeral. In talking with the retirement center director where he had lived, he had quite a few friends and they really want to have a little service. In more normal times, I may have been angrier, less automatic, more defiant towards my now having to be responsible for this after years of not seeing him, more reluctant to take on the tasks of his final tribute. But the irony of his request is lost in the robotic actions that are currently driving me. Years of compartmentalizing grows into an automatic response. In the middle of a trauma, you do, you don't think and you don't feel. That is what I am doing now, taking care of the task assigned to me. I am sure I will have to deal with the emotional fallout at a later date.

After several lengthy calls and extended explanations and pleadings I get everything lined up for a couple of days for now. It is only about a hundred miles, which is fortunate in that Bode's lawyer somehow manages to get permission for Bode to attend. My dad is a source of contention for Bode and me, a topic we generally just avoid. But I know he would want to be there.

With arrangements made and a couple of days to pass, the void of activity and distraction starts to weigh heavily on me. When the mind is not occupied with constructive activity it tends to drift into the realm of obsessive analysis. That is where I find myself now, going round and round without a solution to problems that only exist in the past, yet play in my memory like they are still happening.

The events of the evening, from the first moments in the library to Mike's kiss, play forward and backward in my mind. And with each run through, the unsettling possibility that this was not a random, unfortunate for me, incident looms larger and larger. Maybe it is just a new bent towards paranoia to match my apparent new predisposition to panic attacks. I don't want to believe it was planned. For it to be random means it was just dumb luck that won't repeat itself. For it to be on purpose means someone has been watching me, looking into my life, spending time thinking about how to harm me, to manipulate me, to control me. Random things can happen in life. For someone to deliberately take control of my life is far more unsettling. I don't give up control to anyone and yet these people have managed to take it away from me. I suddenly feel even more vulnerable, if that is even possible.

So far, I have managed to not at all distract myself from things nor come up with an effective plan for the rest of the day. Hiding out in the house with the blinds drawn is extremely tempting. But that seems fraught with the strong possibility that the day would include a trip to the local ABC store for a bottle of my favorite calming elixir. Talk about pouring kerosene on a bonfire. Nope, not a good plan.

I come up with another one instead - one that surprises me as much as anything of the last twenty-four hours. But after all that has happened in the last couple of days, should I really be all that shocked?

Chapter 25

Within a couple of hours I am standing outside in the sunshine. The roar of a high performance car engine whines nearby. All around is a soft breeze and bright yellow warmth from the sun. But I still feel a chill. Maybe it is just the after effects of the night before.

Or maybe it is the fact that Mike is standing next to me. I don't know why I felt inclined to call him. I don't know why I feel so drawn to him, as if I know him from another place, another lifetime. Maybe it is just the intensity of our first encounters. Maybe it is my incessant need to rescue wounded people. Maybe it is that my emotional fortitude, my determined isolationist approach to life is weakened at the moment.

A black Lotus Exige races by, the sun blinding as it reflects off the perfect shine. The grin on Mike's face grows with each lap the car completes. It takes a few minutes as it is a road track, about a two mile loop. But when you are doing 110 miles per hour through the curves, it doesn't take much time.

While we wait, I decide, despite wanting to forget everything about the night a gun was pointed at me and my best friend, I need to know what is happening on the case. "So any leads on those assholes?"

"Not yet. But we'll get them. Put the sketch out. Still on the lookout for your car too."

A knot comes up in stomach as bile burns the back of my throat. The images of the night flash through my brain with all of the same powerful emotions of that night. I fold my arms so as not to show my shaking hands.

"The guy who hit me said his boss said they weren't allowed to hurt me. What the hell does that mean?"

"Um, exactly what it means I'd say. But it does beg the question why. You are sure you didn't recognize either one of them?"

I close my eyes, searching my memory banks. Nothing. "Why wouldn't they kill Michele and me? It's not like they have qualms about murder. They shot that guy at the bar and didn't miss a beat."

"Maybe someone was watching out for you. Any ideas?"

I don't generally associate with the type of people who do this kind of thing. I run across them at work as I have to take out the bullets and stitch up the knife wounds. But I can't imagine anyone keying in on me from that. While I have pissed off my fair share of people, I can't think of anyone who would be so pissed as to set all this up. But then a sudden realization pops out from the milieu of thoughts. "Oh my God, I remember where I saw that guy. Up at a bar near the prison. I was coming back from visiting my brother."

Mike cocks an eyebrow. Processing the possibilities. "You're sure?"

"Well, stake my life on it sure, no. But I'm pretty certain that is where I saw him before. It's been bugging me."

Mike whips his cell phone out and taps a couple of times. "I'll get Charlie, my partner, to run a sketch up there and ask around. What bar was it?"

I give him the directions as the Lotus comes screeching by. Mike turns away to lessen the noise so he can have a conversation.

My heart is beating a little faster than usual, and a little harder. I'd like to pretend it is all about the cars and the speed. But it is more the unsettling feeling that I was not a random victim in all of this. Which leaves the enormous question why.

Mike turns back as the Lotus comes screeching to a stop nearby. He, stands next to me, looking like a little boy on Christmas. "How about we forget about business for now?"

I nod my head, trying to convince myself more than him that I can forget. "Absolutely. It is all about fun now."

"So how do you get to do this? Isn't this place restricted club access? Do you have a sweet little racing car stashed somewhere around here you haven't told me about?" He is practically jumping up and down from the excitement of that thought being possible. Girls with fast cars or cool guns seem to have a powerful effect on guys.

"Calm down, big boy. I don't. But I know how to get us into one."

"Sweet. I didn't entirely believe you when you called, but I am now a dedicated believer."

"The guy who owns this place wrecked a couple of years back. I saved his life and he was so grateful he invited me here. Kept insisting in fact until I took him up on it. Then I saw the light and I come here for a fix every once in a while."

"Nothing like speed and power under you." There's that grin again.

"So I found out. You would think after scraping him up, I would steer clear. No pun intended. But I guess I have that surgeon mentality to laugh death and mayhem in the face. Plus it is just stinking fun."

"So, he lets you use his car?"

"He's got a bunch. The club members all have their own cars they bring down to ride the track, but he has several he will loan out to special people."

"It's good to be special."

I laugh at his enthusiasm. "Yes, it is. And in fact, my favorite of his is the Corvette Zr1. It's a bit flashy—ugly bright yellow but with the view from the inside, it doesn't matter to me. "

"Passenger seat?"

I wrinkle my brow and give him an "are-you-crazy?" look.

"That's okay. It will be fun to watch you have some fun after everything." He looks downright crestfallen. Like his Christmas present was nothing of what he wanted. Pure disappointment poorly masked by an effort to be polite.

"No, you ding – dong. You aren't going to be the passenger. You are the driver."

"What? Are you kidding? Really? No way."

"Can you ask me any other way if I am serious?" I can't help but laugh and he joins me, a big belly laugh. I like a man who can just give off a good laugh and not just a puny ha-ha. "Of course, I go first."

"Always. Ladies first."

With that Barry pulls up in the 'Vette. The rumble of the engine feels like an acoustic massage. He climbs out, an older guy, clearly well off. Slacks. Preppy sweater.

"Here you go, girl. Helmet is in the front seat."

Rules of the course require all cars have a racing harness for the driver and that drivers wear a racing helmet. And that they sign a waiver.

Mike steps back and waves out his arm, a slight bow, beckoning me to the car. "After you, Madam Speed Demon."

I grin. Pause for a moment as I lock my gaze with his. Something passes between us. What I don't know, but I know I like it. But not as much as I like to go fast. So I head to the car. Pull on my helmet. Slide behind the wheel. Close the door. Rev the engine and peel out. Sometime speed kills. Sometime speed heals.

Chapter 26

There is something about too much adrenaline that can lower a person's guard. Whether it is adrenaline born of fear or pleasure, it seems to steal all of one's energy leaving the heart defenseless and vulnerable. That is where I now find myself.

After the stress of the break out, the emotional vulnerability with Dan, the unexpected ghosts in the form of my father and the rush of energy from driving at illegal speeds in a sweet car, I find myself disturbingly open to Mike. Even as it is happening, somewhere in my mind is a quiet voice saying "Stop. Shut up. Run away."

It's a quiet voice and fading fast as we head back to my house. Not a lot of conversation occurs. We are almost both too breathless from the excitement of the driving and of what we both know is about to happen to speak.

Primal urges and instincts have taken over from all rational thought as we strip each other's clothes off even as the front door is still swinging shut. Furiously trying to bury myself in the heat of his kiss and his embrace, we smack into walls and nearly fall onto a heap going up the stairs before finally landing safely on the bed.

What follows is a complete release of all of the pent up emotions, fears, anxieties, longings and heartache of the last days, maybe the last years. I've cut myself off from most people for a long time now. For me Dan had satisfied a physical need. Before him, Scott had been a place I thought I could be safe forever. Turned out I was wrong. After that, I just don't take that risk. Either to harm another or to destroy myself. Building and maintaining the walls takes a toll. How much I haven't realized before, but I am beginning to.

As I fall asleep in Mike's arms, listening to the soft in and out of his breath, feeling it ruffle my hair ever so slightly as his head rests against mine, I refuse to give any credence to the nagging doubts and persistent impulse to run away. More than that I long to wake up in someone's arms. To feel safe and wanted and treasured, even if that feeling is a momentary illusion.

But somewhere inside I know that a feeling like this is always a temporary state of being. I felt it with Scott. I woke up every day for over a year, feeling that warmth, that security. I believed it would last even as I knew I was tearing it apart. Until he finally walked out, full of anger and resentment, taking a piece of my heart along with him, never to be seen again. I shouldn't really blame him. But that doesn't keep me from doing so.

My head swirls with all the memories of past relationships. I have proven incapable of sustaining a relationship with a man. In some way, I mostly destroyed each. One through my inability to give up the bottle. Another through my inability to be vulnerable again. How can I expect this relationship, begun under such bizarre and intense circumstances to turn out any differently? The shouting match in my brain is deafening, arguing over staying or running, afraid to risk the pain but longing to feel the joy.

Sheer exhaustion finally sets in and drives the memories, the emotions to the far corners of my subconscious and I drift off into a quiet and peaceful sleep. And surprisingly, in that last moment of awareness, I dare to have the full thought that just maybe, this time I could make it work and I could be happy. This time I could be different. Maybe the argument has been settled.

Chapter 27

So often in life, things seem crystal clear in the excitement of the moment, in the aftermath of a really good day. One can fall to sleep completely convinced of the truth and reality of something only to awaken in the morning with the dreadful realization that none of it is true.

That is what I would usually expect today. But surprisingly, it is not how I feel when I awaken. For me, this is unknown territory. But the idea of being with Mike, being open and honest and vulnerable seems to be the right thing. It is so out of character for me, I wonder if it is some cosmic communication telling me now is the time, that this is the right man. Or maybe I am just tired of running, tired of hiding and want to believe in some kind of cosmic inevitability to keep the nagging doubts at bay.

I am busily making scrambled eggs and toast for breakfast when Mike strolls out of the bedroom. My heart actually picks up its pace for a moment, a mixture of nervous excitement and passion. His hair is tussled. Wearing just boxers, he seems so comfortable in his own skin. So unassuming. So unaware of how damn hot he looks right now, his trim torso tight, with just a little soft curly hair on his chest.

The pop of the toast out of the toaster shocks me out of my daytime fantasy. He laughs as I startle at the sound.

"Still a bit wound up, I guess?" Stepping up behind me, he wraps his arms around my waist and kisses me gently on the neck. "Hmm, you smell nice."

"That is probably the toast. And yes, it is entirely possible that I have developed PTSD from those assholes."

I turn to face him as our lips instinctively find each other. We share a good morning kiss befitting the night before. All thoughts stop for a moment before I pull away.

"Hey, don't make me burn the eggs!" I grab the spatula and push the eggs around the pan. "Hope you are a breakfast person. If not, then there is coffee. I won't be offended if that is all you want."

"Are you crazy? Breakfast is the best meal of the day. And I'm starved."

It is disarmingly comfortable as we sit across the breakfast table from each other, like it was just another day in a lifetime of days together.

Casual chitchat comes easily. He tells me a little more about himself. A finally normal conversation that we haven't yet had time to share. We avoid the weightiness of discussing his time in the Marines. Instead we stick to the important but mostly emotionally neutral biographical stuff. Son of a cop. Married once for ten years to his high school sweetheart. Has a 14-year-old daughter from the marriage. She lives with her mom but visits on weekends and in the summer. Spends most of his time working but does like to be doing anything that involves being outdoors. Oh yeah, and driving fast. He grins at this last fact, not truly a revelation, reliving the rush of the day before.

"So I guess as a cop you can drive as fast as you want whenever you want, right?" I ask with a wink and a smile.

"Never. I have to be a role model." He says this with a straight face.

"Really? Never? Even when you a late picking up your daughter?"

A slight upturn of the corner of his mouth. "Well, okay but that is an emergency, so allowable."

"Never when you just want to bust out and haul down the highway at ninety just because you can?"

A pause. A grin. Busted. "Damn Kate, you are ruining my carefully crafted image as a pillar of the community."

I roll my eyes, burst out laughing. For these moments, I have forgotten all about the world outside. The gun, the threats, the panic, the death. I wish it could last forever.

Mike grows serious. "So tell me more about yourself. You are nifty at changing the subject, but not anymore. What makes you tick? Who are you, Kate McCullough?"

I turn to look out the window. A bird perches just outside on the thin branch of a dogwood tree just beginning to blossom. His earnestness, his kindness, his intensity all call to me. A resolution within forms. This time I will be true.

I stand up and grab hold of the dishes. This is not a conversation I can have perched across the table from him, having him stare into my eyes, see directly into my soul. I can share my pain, but I cannot let him see where it lives.

"It's not the prettiest of stories."

He doesn't flinch or turn away or question. I steal a glance over at him. Even from the distance of ten feet from the table, his eyes speak, encouraging me to go on, as if he recognizes that vague revelation is simply the tip of the iceberg.

I lean up against the counter, staring past him, still watching the bird. "As you know, my father is dead. He was a heavy drinker and walked out when I was little. My mother lives in town but we are not close. I used to drink a lot too. My drinking was too much for her to take after she watched my father drink his life away. I've changed but amends are not as easy to make as we want them to be. I have one brother, Bode. You saw his picture the other night. He is six years younger than me. We always watched out for each other. He did a better job at it than me. . It cost him everything."

Mike now stands up and come to lean over the bar counter which divides the breakfast nook from the kitchen. His gaze is intense, yet gentle. "In what way?" he asks.

I look towards him, hold his eyes for a moment. I have shared this with only one other person in my life. Not with Michele, not with Dan. Only with Scott. He said it was my drinking; that he couldn't deal with the mood swings, the late nights hanging out at the bar, the irritability. But he never left me until after I came clean with him. After I told him about that night. After that he grew more distant, less patient. Until it was just all over one day. Ever since then I have carried it silently. Unwilling to trust someone with it and unwilling to lose someone over it. That is about to change. And it needs to. I need to.

I find myself lost in this tangent from the past for a few moments. Mike waits patiently for me to go on. The memory of the relief I had initially felt in sharing it with Scott pushes me forward, urges me to take that leap again and trust that Mike's arms will be there to catch me.

"Bode is in prison for manslaughter. For a DUI. But it wasn't really his fault; it was mine. It is only a technicality that the law didn't see it that way."

"How so?"

I try to look at him, to hold his eyes in my own, to open my soul to his. It is too scary and I look away but I press on.

"I was in med school, in between sessions. Home for a few weeks. We went to a party together. Old friends from high school who still lived out in the country, who lived for weekend parties, hanging out in the Duncan's barn. I was the designated driver. We had a deal. Only one of us would drink. It was my turn to pass. Bode was off with a girl he really liked, having a good time. He never really was one to get hammered but he could throw back a few beers."

Suddenly I am fully back in those moments. The music, the laughter, the keg of beer. Someone breaks out the Jack Daniels and the shot glasses. It burns so good on the way down. Just one. Okay, maybe two. It's just a little, no big deal. I need another beer though. The pizza just isn't as good without the beer to wash it down. Dancing with Patrick, one of my brother's friends. He is so hot and I am so insecure. The beer, the shots let me loose, let me be free.

Bode finds me. It is getting late. We have to get back to pick up mom from her second shift at the hospital. She is a nurse. Has worked second shift for years to bring in the extra money. Her car was in the shop and we were her ride.

"What the hell, Kate? You're falling over drunk." Bode is mad. But I don't care. I love the way alcohol makes me feel, makes me forget, makes me not afraid of everything, of being hurt by someone.

"I'm sorry, Bode. It was just a couple. I'm good." I jingle the keys at him, wave him to the exit. "Let's go. It's all good."

"It's not good, Kate. You are not driving like that." He snatches the keys. I leap up, trying to grab them back. He is six inches taller and a lot steadier on his feet. I miss the keys and instead stumble up against him. "Bode, you can't drive. You had a drink. I saw you." I say this singsong, as if it is some secret I discovered. How stupid I can be when I am drunk.

He glances around at the few remaining, less than sober, friends. "Maybe we can get a cab to come out."

I burst out laughing. "A cab? We are in the middle of a field in the middle of nowhere. Who are you gonna call? 1-800-pick-up-a-cow?"

Bode is just getting angrier. We both know Mom will go off if we don't pick her up because we are off at a party drinking. Alcohol is her fire point. Not surprising given my Dad's history with it.

"Kate, mom will fucking kill us if we don't show."

I chime in "Or if we show up with a designated driver name Joe." I laugh, finding this entirely too funny in a completely unfunny situation.

"Damn it Kate. I can't believe you did this again. I drank a hell of a lot less then you, so I guess I'm driving. Let's go. " He grabs my hand and pulls me behind him. I wave weakly at Patrick as we disappear out of the barn and into the dark.

Mike has not said a word as I describe the scene. With Scott, I never shared all the details, although I have replayed them hundreds of time in my mind. I am not sure why I am sharing them now. It is as if the story has demanded to be told at this moment, in full detail, with full disclosure. I am briefly aware of this sensation as I slip back into that other place and time in my head.

It is so dark tonight. Cloudy with no moon. Empty countryside, empty roads for most of the trip. We are coming up to the outskirts of town. A few scattered houses set far back from the road, too far out of town for streetlights. I am slumped down in the back seat, watching the trees whisk by, bizarrely fascinated with a simple phenomenon in my drunken stupor.

A sudden screech of tires. Bode yells. I fly across the back seat as the car swerves. A sickening thud as the front window spiders. We come to a stop off the side of the road in a ditch. The airbag has exploded in Bode's face. I lay on the back floor, draped over the center hump like a sack of potatoes.

"Oh fuck, fuck," Bode is yelling. I pop my head up as he tears away the limp fabric draping over his lap.

128

"What the hell was that Bode?" I say it like only a clueless drunken asshole can say it.

"I hit somebody. Come on. We gotta help him." With that he slides out the door and disappears.

Through the fog of alcohol, I gain some sense of myself. The sudden jolt of adrenaline from the crash does serve to clear my brain for a moment as I comprehend what he said. "Holy shit." I jump out of the car to join him.

I have to stop as the world spins for a moment. I think it is less because of the booze coursing through me and more due to the scene in front of me. A man, lying in a pool of blood. A bloodied jagged cut on his head. His leg twisted grotesquely under him, blood pouring from a huge open wound. I think I can see bone which makes me want to hurl. Bode is leaning over him, hesitant, unsure what to do. His face contorted with fear and horror. I need to take the lead. I am the med student. I should know what to do.

CPR. Start with the ABC's. I have at least learned the basics. I can do this. I kneel beside Bode, feel for a pulse, look for any signs of breathing, of life. There is none, but he is still warm. His blood his still pouring out of his wounds. I start CPR. One-two-three-four. Bode looks at me, fear shines off his face like a beacon in a storm.

"Put pressure on his leg Bode. We have to stop the bleeding or the CPR won't help at all." My voice is shrill and quivering, not at all conveying the calm collected medical provider I want to be. No, instead it tells of my terror and horror at the scene that I am now a part of, acting but on the edge of panic.

Bode obediently places his hands over the leg wound. We are both covered in blood. How can one man give off so much blood? It is all I can do to channel my adrenaline into something useful. I want to run away screaming but I don't. One-two-three. The regular steady counting of CPR helps me focus.

Across the field a light flickers on as someone in a nearby house comes out to investigate the sounds, the squeal of tires, the crash of the windshield.

Bode shouts out "Call 911. We hit a guy with the car."

I look at him. Don't say that. Don't tell them we did it, I want to scream. But what's the point of that?

"Shit Kate, I am so fucked."

I don't stop doing CPR but I can tell it is pointless. The man's lips are blue, his arm is cool as it presses up against my leg. "No Bode, me. Not you. Me. I was driving."

He looks at me, tears streaming down his face. I can already see the bruise coming up and the abrasion on his cheek where the airbag hit him. "No, Kate. That's stupid. It was me, my fault. They'll know anyway." His voice suddenly sounds so sad to me, a frightened and lonely child.

It seems like eternity and an instant before the police come screaming up, lights and sirens. The ambulance is close behind. I step back as the EMT's take over. The police have taken Bode aside and are talking to him. What are they saying? What is Bode telling them? I stand alone, covered in blood, my mind blank and filled with thoughts all at once. We didn't mean it, I want to tell them. It wasn't his fault. I was supposed to be driving. I shake my head to clear my thoughts.

Only I really am shaking my head, trying to shake the images out, trying to come back to the current moment. Mike with his arms around me, tears streaming down my face, my body shivering from the release of emotions. I thought the memories would fade with time, but it is as if giving voice to them as brought them back to life. Several minutes pass without a word between us, just one heart clinging to another in the tumult of life.

Chapter 28

The naked emotional intimacy of the morning leaves me completely exhausted and strangely more at peace than I have been in a long time. Maybe releasing the story into the universe with sound provides some cosmic healing. Maybe the possibility that this time it can be different, that I can be different in a relationship actually takes a firm hold in my brain.

Mike has what I can only describe as an unfazed reaction. No look of judgment, horror, disappointment, anger or fear. No bizarre effort to brush it away as insignificant or unimportant. He simply lets me tell the story. And in the end, the hug is really the most effective way to soothe me, to make me feel he has not left me because of what I have done.

As the emotions settle, I get back to cleaning up the breakfast fallout, Mike at my side. Again it feels strangely normal. After moments of silence, which seems like an appropriately needed space, he picks up in the easy curious questioning of learning more about me as though just carrying on with the conversation.

"So what are things like with your brother now?"

I slide the last couple of rinsed dishes into the dishwasher. "Close. Even closer."

Mike scrubs the last of the scrambled eggs from the pan. "So do you get to visit him much or does your schedule prevent that?"

I wipe my wet hands on the dishtowel and toss it onto the counter. Cleaning finished. "Every chance I get. But usually ends up

131

just being once a month. We write letters. Old fashioned I know, but he doesn't exactly get free access to email."

"When does he get out?"

"Probation hearing in three months. I think he'll get it. He's a good person and has made the best of being in prison."

"Best of being in prison. That sounds pretty bleak. So does he have buddies or does he mostly keep to himself?"

"Bode is mister social. He can talk to anyone, anywhere, anytime. So yeah, I guess you could say he has some friends if that's what you want to call them. I think he does what he needs to in order to get by and do his time without trouble. He can make the best of any situation."

It is hard to describe Bode in the context of being in prison. It has confined him and stifled him in so many ways, but at the same time, Bode is the freest soul I know. No matter how deep the shit around him, he can always find the goodness, always see a way through without betraying who he is. It is how he could forgive me for the accident. It is why it is so much harder for me to forgive myself. I deserve to be punished and Bode is not going to be the one to do it.

"So I guess you would do anything for your brother, huh?"

I cock my head, give it some thought. Not towards the answer, but towards the question. Why does he ask it when to me, the answer is so obvious. "Yeah, anything. He's my little brother. I'd give him my life if need be."

Mike contemplates this for moment. "I don't have a brother or sister but I guess it is no different than what I would do for my daughter."

As he finishes toweling off the frying pan, I give him a big hug from behind. "There are people in life that just mean that much. We do what we have to in order to protect them."

He turns, bends down to deliver a kiss. I openly dive into his deep passion, feeling safer and more secure than I have in a long time. How ironic it has come on the heels of such fear and danger. And even as I feel like this feeling could last forever, I know that nothing stays still, everything is in motion and even the best feelings can be ripped away in the reality that is life.

Chapter 29

Mike has to go into work. I can't bring myself to do the same. Not that I avoid all things unpleasant and painful. I call my mother to let her know of Dad's passing. It is a disjointed, awkward conversation. To say things are strained between my mother and me is a grand understatement. We were always a bit like oil and water, me taking after my dad, that fact creating a predisposition towards resentment in my mother. She loved my dad once upon a time. And she loves me. Of this I do not doubt. But just because you love someone, doesn't mean you like much of who they are. And I made it really hard for my mom to like me. My fondness of alcohol and my tendency to make stupid choices resulted in her bailing me out of trouble a lot. Over time it created a barrier between us.

The barrier grew into the Great Wall of China after the accident. Her son is in prison and even though we never talked about it, she knew I was responsible for the events of that night. Some things even a mother has a hard time forgiving. Love can exist even where forgiveness cannot. But it creates a confusing and frustrating relationship.

I invite her to attend the memorial service with us. She seems to consider it for a moment, more because of the opportunity to see Bode than a chance to honor the man she shared her home with for sixteen years. The ensuing twenty destroyed any good memories I suspect. In the end, she declines. We promise each other to meet for dinner sometime soon, both knowing the unlikelihood of that actually happening. At least not until Bode is out. He will make us sit down together, to be a family, to find a way through the anger and disappointment.

I decide to take a ride up to see Bode. I am sure his lawyer has made him aware of Dad's death and the plan for the memorial service taking place tomorrow. While I wanted to tell Bode in person, getting his lawyer to get him released was more important and we couldn't wait on me to get up there to see Bode. And even though I would see him tomorrow, I needed to go today. Just to fill the time I tell myself. But even I don't believe that to be true, and I'm not even sure why it needs to be.

I give Michele a call while I am driving up. She is still pretty rattled by the events of the week and unlike me, she has no need to prove herself by diving right back into work and walking the same halls that were not so long ago filled with terror for both of us. She is taking the kids and going up to visit her mother up in Ohio for a while. A pang of jealousy courses through me, the unacknowledged but ever present wish to have a family to retreat to making itself known. A wish for safe travels and an expression of love for her and the kids and I am back to the solitary quiet cocoon of the car.

I wonder a bit about Davis. His wound really did look bad, so he could be in rough shape by now. Is it actual worry I feel for him? Or just clinical curiosity about what happened to him? Maybe I am just mad that one of my patients has developed an infection. That does annoy me more than anything about the whole situation. It was a dirty wound made by a filthy blunt shank. Hardly an unexpected development despite using antibiotics. But it still feels a bit like I failed.

A craving for a drink. Not unusual, especially when I am stressed. But unusually fleeting as my mind quickly moves onto thinking about Mike. I am stunned, in a good way, of how he has accepted me, taken in all that I shared and has not pulled away like a person stumbling upon a grotesque, deformed corpse in the house of someone they are visiting. To me, this is much more than a skeleton in the closet. Rather, it still contains the foul smell of something just nearly alive, just recently dead. I think it will always be that way. At least I have until now.

Bode looks a bit worn and worried when he comes into the visitation room. I give him a peck on the cheek before we sit down.

"How are you doing?" We say it at the same moment. It has happened a hundred times before and usually brings a smile. But not this time. We are both on edge.

"You first." He nods towards me.

"No, you. I know you must be upset about Dad." Bode and I have long had a different perspective on our father. As usual, he is far more forgiving and accepting. So I know the news of his death is hard on him.

"Yeh. But it's not like…" His voice cracks and fades. I am not sure if it is simple grief or more a holding of something back. His next words point the way. "Kate, he had a bad heart. I knew something like this could happen anytime."

I can't hide the astonishment and confusion in my expression. One of the many reasons I suck at poker. "What?" Anything more specific than that escapes me at the moment.

"He's been going downhill." Bode can't look at me.

But I stare straight at him. "What are you talking about? How would you know that?"

"We have kept in touch. He writes. Has called a couple of times. Even saw him before I went away."

My emotions swirl like the little vortexes of sand that kick up in high wind in the desert. Jealousy, anger, disappointment, confusion, relief. All mixed together with no clear winner.

"Why? Why didn't you tell me? Why didn't you tell me where he was?"

Bode's face cannot mask his guilt, his wish that I understand, that I not hold it against him. "Because he asked me not to. He didn't want you to know."

My face flushes with anger. Even after his death, my father has managed to commit one more act of selfishness against me. "I am his daughter. I had a right to know before the day he died."

Bode covers my hand with his but I pull away, fists balled in anger. Why am I angry? Why am I surprised? My father said he was watching. But how could he have reached out to Bode and not to me?

Bode lets the silence sit for a moment. "He knew he had screwed up badly. That he had ruined your life. He didn't want to cause you any more pain."

"That's such a load of self-righteous crap couched in noble sacrifice. He didn't have the guts to face me. He ran away like a coward. He couldn't face me because he wasn't strong enough to fight the same demon I do every day. Only after he knew he was dying, when he wanted my forgiveness could he face me."

It is Bode's turn to sit back, to contemplate my viewpoint. I wipe away a stray tear that has found its way onto my cheek. Is it grief or fury or deep pain that gave birth to the tear? The mind is too complex, too mysterious in its emotions to know for certain.

Several moments pass, each of us trapped in a separate space within ourselves. Finally, with a deep breath, I shake free of the emotions, regain some distance, some detachment. "I'm sorry. I'm not mad at you. You did what he asked." I say it even as I am trying to make myself entirely believe it. Fake it till you make it.

This time I reach for Bode's hand. It strikes me that it looks like my father's hand. I had never realized that before. The death of a loved one brings weird, incongruous completely unexpected thoughts. Bode looks up at me, pats my hand with his free one. Our hands now stacked like playing Slap Jack. The physical link between our souls.

"No Kate. I'm sorry. I didn't know what to do. I wanted to tell you but he made me promise not to. But I just can't lie to you anymore."

I pull my hands away, wipe my face, pulling my hair back. Sigh heavily. "There is just so much stuff going on right now. And now this. It's just a lot."

An inquisitive expression now on his face, Bode asks "Stuff? What kind of stuff?"

Suddenly aware how I opened the door to the events of the last few days, something I had vowed during the drive up, not to do, I mentally kick myself. I try to keep him out of what goes on in my life – the ups and downs and the scrapes I get into. It isn't exactly hard. Not as if he shows up on my doorstep unannounced. Knowing would just frustrate and scare him. So I don't share.

I try to minimize. "Nothing really. Just some stupid stuff."

That doesn't work. He calls me on it. "Bullshit. Tell."

So I share the events of my life, trying to minimize the actual danger and the fear that I had felt. Hard to do that when there are guns and bad guys in the story. He listens quietly, intently, his face growing angry but tinged with fear.

He says nothing for a few minutes. What is there to say after a story like that? Sorry, that sucks, glad you are okay? All of it seems a bit trite.

So he takes my hand and holds it up to his bowed head, squeezing it as if his mind can enter into me through it. "Thank God."

That's really all that needs to be said. And it's really all I need. Just being able to tell him is enough. The catharsis of it helps restore some sense of balance and control far fleeting in the last few days. We draw strength from each other, although I think it is me drawing more than him mostly. And when nothing else, no one else can help me find solid ground, just talking to Bode can do that.

I leave with the distinct happiness of knowing I will see him tomorrow. A guard will escort him to the service and stand by during it and drive him back. Fortunately the fact that he is not a violent offender and has a great track record in prison makes any of it possible.

On the drive back I am able to focus more, to find some solid footing, resolve to move forward from here. To make better decisions, to be more open to life, to take a chance on being happy. Of course I still make my usual stop at the bar on the way home, trying hard to ignore the nagging little voice that keeps saying things will not turn out well.

Chapter 30

There are a surprising number of people at my father's memorial service. He wanted to be cremated and his ashes spread up in the mountains. He had arranged for a close friend to take care of that. So we just have a small wake at the assisted living facility where he lived.

Apparently, he had found his way to sobriety in the last years, reaching out to help others, to make amends for the mistakes of his past. He was clearly loved by the people here.

Bode looks good in the suit that I had brought up to him yesterday. It is strange to see him in real clothes after so many years of prison orange. With a little effort, I can imagine him free. Free to live his life, to become everything he should be, to do all the good I know he can do in life. Only the shackles on his wrists and the burly guard in the brown uniform, gun on his belt, tells the truth that is otherwise.

Bode is clearly saddened by the death of our father. But knowing him so well, I can also tell he is so relieved and happy to be free from the prison walls, even if for a short time. He is charming and gracious as people give us their condolences. I can't help but notice how little everyone seems bothered by his shackles. Clearly Dad had been sharing his life and those of his kids with these people. And they didn't judge him, or us.

It is a beautiful spring day, even after a chilly start, so we decide to take the remainder of the wake outside to the garden area. The warm yellow glow of the sun on my skin lifts the mood. Person after person introduces himself or herself. Tells me how much my dad spoke of me, how proud he was of me, that I was his doctor daughter. I try to process this image of my father, reconcile it with the one I have carried for so long. It leaves me a bit off balance, like I have entered the Twilight Zone and am now participating in someone else's life.

I hang back from Bode, let him take the lead. But during a lull, he turns towards me.

"How are you holding up, Kate? I know you hate this kind of stuff."

I shrug. "Fine. It's just so weird. The whole thing."

"Tell me about it. If it weren't for the cuffs, I would almost think I had a normal life."

I smile sympathetically. His words cut through to the ever-present guilt I carry. I should be the one in cuffs. Not Bode. I think it. But I can't say it. We have had only a few conversations about it since that night. Me condemning myself, him trying to shoulder the blame, to exonerate me. No matter how hard he tried, he never could. It just added to my guilt and his frustration, so eventually we stopped talking about it.

I shake myself out of the self-indulgent self-loathing and wrap my arm around his shoulder. Kiss him on the cheek. "Soon Bode. Soon you can go anywhere you want, do anything you want. Live your life the way it should have been all along."

He lets the last comment slide by without comment. I am grateful every day to have a brother who is so good hearted as to pay the price for my stupid, selfish mistake and never chastise, never complain. I have never stopped to think that it is his own guilt that drives him. That he may truly believe he belongs in prison. That he is not just saying these things for my benefit, to alleviate my guilt.

That is how it is with the human brain. Sometimes we become so convinced of our view on the world that the possibility of another viewpoint fails to even cross our horizon. For a reason I don't understand, that possibility crosses my mind at this moment. Could it be that his persistent silence on the events of that night are born not out of noble sacrifice but of something darker, his own inner demons, his sense of guilt? And if I haven't seen this in him before, what else have I failed to see?

I let it go by. I have to. The idea of Bode in prison because he should be in prison. Him believing that. It steals away the image I have created of Bode. The one I need to have for my life to make sense.

With this new perspective on Bode bouncing around my brain, along with the exhausting continuous stream of polite niceties, I suddenly feel the need for some space. I squeeze Bode's arm. "Hey, I need a break. You good if I step away?"

He nods, winks. "I'm good. You go."

I slip out of the center of people who are starting to cluster around us once again. As I come around the corner of the building enclosing one side of the courtyard, I come up short. I see the silhouette of a man, square shoulders, close cropped hair, dark suit. He disappears into the main office building. I swear it is Mike. My brain struggles to put it all together, to make sense of his being here, of not telling me he was here. He said he was working today. There is no reason for him to be here. It is the sun and the emotions and the altered reality of today that is just playing tricks on my brain.

Our brain cannot process every little detail we take in with our eyes so it tends to just fill in the missing pieces with familiar things. That is what mine is doing now, putting the familiar, the recently known into the voids left by imperfect senses. Or at least that is what I tell myself

Chapter 31

The following day seems as good as any to get back to a normal life. I am determined to make it so, despite a considerable amount of anxiety over returning to the hospital. How frustrating that the brain holds onto brief experiences as though it will always be true while it takes years to build good habits. Despite the countless monotonous hours of my life spent here, the shadows from the night of fear and violence are everywhere I go.

I need to rebuild my confidence. Stop doubting my ability to deal with whatever comes. I know I handled myself well that night. And I know those assholes are long gone, never to be seen by me again. Yet as I walk through these same hallways in the evening as the sun sets and the visitors thin out, I get a little knot in my stomach, a little quickening of my pulse. It pisses me off to be afraid. Once again my mind argues with my brain to just cut it out and stop being a big baby. It ends pretty much a draw. My brain makes my body feel afraid, while I go about my business as though that is not true.

In the end, it is an uneventful day, exactly what I need. Covered rounds on a couple of patients of another surgeon. Took out a gallbladder full of stones. A few office follow-ups. Traumas are the majority of what I do but don't make me enough to pay the bills. Many of the trauma victims are not the kind of guys who a prompt payers. Usually their payments are made exactly never. When they come in with knife wounds, gunshots and various other intentionally inflicted injuries, I am fairly certain that paying my bill is not their primary concern. I am also fairly certain any effort to get any money out of them is an exercise in folly.

So in the time between the excitement of trauma patients, I get to do run of the mill general surgery stuff. The body has been kind enough to create some spare parts, appendix, gallbladder. Things for the surgeon to take out when they becomes a problem. The only known function of an appendix is paying the mortgage on the surgeon's house.

These patients are a refreshing change from the drama of trauma patients. While someone with appendicitis or a bad gallbladder can be quite ill and suffering, it is usually not quite the same level of emotional intensity as dealing with a trauma patient. When life goes from completely normal to life threatening in an unexpected fashion as happens in traumas, the patients and their families deal in many different ways, some less constructive than others.

It is exactly the kind of boring, nondramatic day I need. By the end, I am exhausted but somewhat relieved to find that I can do this. Maybe I can get on with my life and with my job without a new dark shadow following me around. My preexisting demons are quite enough. Somewhere during the day, I make a decision to not let my experience go to waste, to learn something from it. After all, every experience can be of benefit if we choose to use the lessons learned to make things different. Cliché as it is, it has reminded me of the delicacy and fragility of life.

So in the spirit of seizing the opportunity and not letting the moment pass, I agree to meet Mike for dinner. I am nervous, and it is not just the happy butterflies of new infatuation. It is a deeper anxiety that comes from deep revelation. I shared the deepest, darkest part of my soul and we have not spoken substantially since. Will he still be accepting? Will he have questions? Will he be so horrified after time for reflection that he condemns me? It is "will he still love me tomorrow" taken to a whole new level.

He arrives at my place, Chinese food in hand. Eating in was his idea. I do not know if I find that reassuring or unsettling. Privacy to allow intimacy or privacy to allow chastisement? I am about to find out.

A quick hug and kiss and he drops the food on the counter. A longer, slower, deeper kiss. I open my eyes at the sound of jingling keys. He has reached into his pocket while we kissed and retrieved a set of keys.

"Look what we found." Mike's face lights up when he smiles.

"Oh my God! You found my jeep!" Embarrassing as it is, I actually squeal with delight. "You are the best." I jump back into his arms, wrapping mine around his neck.

"Whoa, whoa, whoa. Don't get too excited yet." He peels my arms down. "Crime scene guys need it for a day to go through it but you can have it after that. Just a day. They already started processing it today. Found some prints."

"Those assholes didn't trash it, did they?" My face turns fierce. While I keep people at arm's length, I attach to inanimate objects easily. I love my Jeep.

"Um. That depends on what kind of shape it was in before they stole it." Mike gives off a giggle as I punch him in his very strong, very firm, very thick arm.

"Hey now, it may be beat up but it is mine. It has character."

"Character? I thought they were called dents and scratches." Another giggle. Another punch.

"Don't forget the rips in the interior. It takes years to get a car to look like that." I say all this with mock sincerity. But in some weird way I do love the vehicle because of the dents and scratches. Maybe it is a reminder of myself. Beat up with a lot of dings but maybe

145

someday I can find someone who loves me because of it or at least in spite of it.

"Come on, let's eat." Mike starts ripping open the bags, pulling out the neat white cartons of food as I pull a couple of plates out of the cabinet. "I'm sorry, I should have brought some wine," he adds casually.

I pause, mid motion, for a moment. My brain scrambles, playing back in high speed, our conversation of the day before. It occurs to me that while I shared what happened that night with Bode, I didn't really go into the ongoing challenge I have with alcohol. Adding more bad news to that seems like just begging for rejection but why stop now? It is my new found philosophy, developed earlier today, to seize the moment and be forthright.

"Well. " I sputter a bit getting started. "It's probably better. I don't drink anymore. Well, more truthful would be, I can't drink anymore. I want to every day, but I can't."

I look over at Mike to gauge his reaction. And just as before, he doesn't flinch, he doesn't turn away. He simply shrugs. "Okay. Then I should say, sorry for not bringing some fruit punch."

Relieved by his nonchalant reply, I burst out laughing. "Fruit punch? Who the hell drinks fruit punch?"

Mike can't hold his laughter either. "Church socials?"

I slide the plates onto the counter next to the open containers. I slip his arms around my waist and hungrily kiss him. "Well, I do not feel like being particularly social right now. And we are definitely not at church."

With that, he lifts me off the ground, holding me tight against his body, his appetite now turned towards nonfood items. Good thing Chinese food reheats well.

Chapter 32

After satisfying one kind of appetite, Mike and I return to addressing the original issue. Namely, we are both famished. In retrospect, I wish we had just stayed in bed. But wish as I might, I have yet to find a way to make life freeze at the good moments. It always marches ahead, sometimes slowly chipping away at happiness, sometimes ripping it away in one devastating rush. Each way brings its own exquisite type of pain.

After polishing off the Sesame Chicken and Lo Mein over some chitchat, Mike grows serious. Instinctively, my back stiffens a little, even though there is no clear menace in his demeanor. A not so random but fleeting thought shoots through my brain. Something along the lines of "Here comes the shoe drop."

But I am also curious as he retrieves a briefcase, which he had carried in, and slips out a file folder. So much for the twenty-first century technology. Paperwork is alive and well in some places.

He clears his throat before beginning. I do not want to make this easy for him although I have no idea why I feel this way. He has consistently been on my side since I met him so I cannot determine my sudden uneasiness, other than long history and hardwired distrust.

"Not to ruin the moment, but I do need to talk to you more about your case." He almost looks sheepish but that is quickly replaced with a hardened business face. It's too late, the moment is ruined.

I do want to give him the benefit of the doubt. Why would discussing what happened be confrontational? I am just over reading his demeanor. I tell myself to stay open to this possibility, this probability. I give a warm smile. "Okay. Seems reasonable. We have been goofing off mostly and it is your job. And I would really like to nail these assholes. Thanks for giving me some space from it for a few days."

He relaxes a little at my smile although does not return it. He almost looks as uncomfortable as I feel. "Good. I figured you needed a little time. I have been working on it though and have a couple of solid leads."

"Great. Have you found them?" I am not sure why I ask this, as I am fairly certain he would have mentioned this to me. "Who are they?"

"Haven't found them. But potentially ID'd the one guy. I think you called him Clean Cut."

"Yeah, he seemed like more of the brains of the group. Of course, that being relative."

Mike gives a slight smirk at my sarcasm. It creeps me out suddenly, reminding me of Clean Cut's smirk. My heart rate picks up a bit. A sense of dread kicks in just a bit. Damn emotional memory. Or is it intuition?

Mike slips a photo out of the file folder and slides it across the table towards me. I recognize him instantly. His hair is a bit longer and he looks like he just came off a bender, a stubbly beard, blood shot eyes. But it is definitely him, Clean Cut.

"That's him. Who is he?"

Mike slides the picture back into the folder. I appreciate the move as looking in that guy's eyes, even if it is just in a picture sends a cold chill down my spine. I can almost feel the gun against my spine, see the terror in Michele's face.

"Name is Max Satterwhite. Bad guy. In and out of trouble most of his life. You are lucky he let you walk away."

A lump in my throat at the implications of that statement. While I have walked around with a quiet fear inside since that night, in some weird way, it also feels like a movie, something outside of myself, the happy ending a given, although long in coming. At the time I did truly believe he would kill both Michele and me, but with time, my brain had made that an ever more remote possibility. Maybe a way of coping, maybe a way of incorporating the event into my reality.

I cannot even come up with a reply, instead becoming aware of the dryness in my mouth and the sweatiness of my palms.

Mike keeps going. "Mostly a gun for hire but lately has been working for a white collar mobster. Boss keeps his hands clean while Max here does the dirty work."

"Nice." A note of sarcasm colors my reply. "So is he working for this same guy on this, whatever this is?"

"Can't say for certain but it seems likely." Mike looks intently into my eyes. I meet his gaze, unflinching. It verges on a staring match until I give in and look away. The sense he is trying to read something behind my eyes is not comforting in this moment. I feel myself withdrawing a little as the tone takes a subtle shift to one more of confrontation and less of consolation.

I can't explain how I can read this kind of shift of attitude. It is not something said, it is not some clear physical gesture. Maybe it is subtle facial expressions, minor shifts in posture. But over time I have proven usually right in reading other people. I wish more than anything that I could be wrong right now, that I am overreacting because of the recent vulnerability and openness and unexpected events. Sometimes being wrong is so right. But I do not have the luxury of being wrong now.

Chapter 33

It may be my imagination, but I swear Mike assumes a more aggressive posture. Leaning forward over the table, shoulders hunched up, jaw tight. He slides another photo out of the folder and pushes it across the table to me.

I don't reach out to take it. In fact, I keep my arms tightly folded across my chest. A defensive posture if there ever was one. I glance at the photo. My mind spins. I know that face. Where do I know him from? It is a middle age, well-groomed white man. It is clearly a mug shot but he looks like he could be sitting for a formal portrait, not a hair out of place. God, he looks so familiar but I can't quite place him.

I look up at Mike who is studying me closely, searching for a sign of something. What I am not sure. "Know him?" He cocks his head slightly.

I still can't place him. So I tell him the truth. "No." Why don't I go on to say he looks familiar, how I may know him from somewhere but can't say where? Is it some instinct towards a need for self-preservation? Or just my being stubborn?

Mike presses. "Are you sure?"

I dig in my proverbial heels. "No. I don't."

I am definitely not wrong about the shifting atmosphere.

"You said you are still close with your brother, right? That you visit him regularly?"

A little heat comes into my face; my look becomes more of a glare. "You know I am. I told you that." The image of my brother floats into my consciousness and with it, another face pops up. The man in the photo. I do know him.

"So you see your brother all the time. You know all about what is going on with him. But you don't know Stephen Samson. Your brother's protection in prison."

I sit back as if blasted by a cannon. A vague picture of where this is going is starting to form. "Protection? Yeah, I do recognize the guy. But it is just some guy Bode knows in prison. There are only so many friends you can make in a place like that." I fall back on my sarcasm for defense. But it occurs to me that claiming I did not know him until Mike gave me a hint sounds truly lame and deliberately untruthful, true as it is.

"Maybe they are more than casual prison buddies. Maybe they have something going on together on the outside." Mike grows more aggressive, more accusatory in his tone.

My brain is reeling, trying to find something solid to hang onto. It feels like my world is suddenly spinning out of control, even more so than in the last few days if that is possible. I can feel my lip quiver, the pressure in my chest that comes with the sudden urge to cry. I refuse. I fight it. I will not let this man get the best of me. He has once already, making me trust him, open up to him, but not again. Not like this.

I summon anger and hostility to my aide. "What the hell are you saying, Mike?"

Mike slides a mug shot of my brother out of the folder and places it beside the first picture. "This is what I could see happening. Bode and this guy Stephen Samson have something going on the outside. Bode asks you for a favor. You owe him a debt you can't repay. You said it yourself. So you help him out. Who could blame you?"

My mind suddenly goes completely silent. My body, completely still. Lost in the pain of betrayal and anger at myself for being vulnerable, everything crystallizes in my thinking. It all makes sense. He manipulated me and now is using my own words against me. The intense hurt, the betrayal cuts so deep that it unleashes a fury from deep within.

I push the photos away, and stand up from the table. My chair pushes violently outwards, tipping dangerously backwards before righting itself. All the tears are gone. Nothing but white-hot anger burns inside. But rather than yelling, my voice is icy calm. "You let me open my heart to you. To share something I have never shared with anyone else." Not entirely true, but close enough to allow for my point. "All the while you are just working me, looking for an angle. And then you use my own words to accuse me of this. Of breaking a scumbag out of jail. Of risking the life of my best friend. Of being so stupid as to destroy my life for some asshole I don't know. What kind a fucking bastard are you?"

Mike spreads his arms, softens his expression, attempting to some convey some kind of innocence or regret. "I wasn't playing you Kate. I really care about you. I just found all this out yesterday morning. I'm just trying to make sense of it."

"Yesterday morning?" I pause, recalling the figure I saw at my father's service. I thought it was Mike. It couldn't be I had told myself. It wouldn't be. But it was. "It was you. It was you I saw up at my Dad's service yesterday afternoon. You were there to fucking spy on me and my brother." I can feel my face flush with red heat. It feels as though someone has stuck a stiletto through my heart. "You bastard."

The name-calling seems so inadequate. Words in general seem so useless in expressing my hurt and my anger. Mike's shrug only makes me seethe more.

A moment of silent rage swirls around us. Mike stands up. Tries to approach. I take a step back.

"Kate, it's my job. I just need to know the truth. Just tell me. We can deal with whatever it is."

This proclamation does nothing to settle me. In fact the idea that he believes it could be true just feels like a twist of the stiletto. I can't breathe. I feel like the walls are suddenly closing in. I take a deep breath to regain some control. "IT is nothing." I put a hard emphasis on the "it". " I had nothing to do with it. Bode had nothing to do with it. I don't know what this guy Samson has to do with it, but it is just a coincidence that he knows my brother."

That last thought bounces around my head for a fleeting moment. Is it just a coincidence? I know Bode wasn't involved. That is not who he is. He doesn't even belong in prison. But what if he thinks he does? Does that change things, change him? These are not thoughts I am ready to share with Mike.

Mike stands perfectly still. An unreadable expression on his face. It is not clear to me if he actually accepts my answer. Or if he is waiting for a full confession. He must be a hell of a poker player.

My anger gives birth to full blown cutting sarcasm. "Is this how you interrogate all your suspects Detective Morgan? You fuck them into a confession?"

Mike's face darkens, a hint of anger permeates it. "That's not fair, Kate. I just got all this information. I just need to know the truth. You have to know our being together wasn't about this."

"Do I? How would I? I don't know who the hell you are. And I was a damn fool to ever think I did."

He reaches out, tries to touch my arm. I rip it away.

"What the hell do you want from me, Kate? I care about you. I think I could love you. But I can't do my job with my dick."

My mouth opens with disbelief. "Love? Care? That's rich." There is so much I could say right now. So much I want to say. But I can't. I don't. I don't want to admit out loud how much he has hurt me. I just want to get away from him. To erase the last few days when I trusted him, when I opened myself to him, when I dared believe I could find, might deserve to find, happiness in this life.

All I say is this. "Well you can't do me anymore either. So get the hell out of my house. Now."

Chapter 34

The night is worthless. I pace around the house for most of it. I want a drink so badly but don't want to see anyone, speak to anyone. So I stay in, where there is no alcohol. This is the reason I have none in the house. It would be too easy. A battle I would be sure to lose. Instead, I clean the place from top to bottom, pitching out piles of stuff, some trash, some good stuff. I just feel the need to purge. Maybe it is a symbol. Maybe it is just a way to have some sense of control.

I'm without my Jeep until tonight so I have to beg a ride from a neighbor. Fortunately, it is only a short ride to the hospital and he is able to drop me off on his way to work. A surgeon can only live but so far from the hospital before being able to respond to calls in a reasonable amount of time becomes problematic. I am sure I can beg a ride over to the police department later to get my Jeep. I have already called to confirm I can get it on my way home. I just pray I do not run into Mike.

The day at work is mostly a blur. I am sure I am abrasive and short with most everyone I talk to. I am not usually the moody surgeon but in this case, the stereotype works for me and I let it ride. I will make amends tomorrow, or next week, or next month. It may be a while before I can be nice or kind or patient or understanding with anyone. I wish Michele were here. She can always talk me down. Help me see the bigger picture and let go of things. But she is not. She is off with her family, her children. Am I jealous, resentful? How confusing to feel those things mixed in with love.

Upon returning home, I once again feel the walls closing in. I go for a run. Rather than draining the energy that is feeding the anger, it seems to just fuel it on. Every pounding foot step accents a curse word in my brain. Most of them directed at Mike. Some at myself for being so stupid as to trust someone. To allow someone behind the walls. Even after the run and a shower, I can't sit still. I feel like a caged animal pacing around, needing some kind of release.

I grab my keys, head out the door and drive straight to my place of centering. Probably not the wisest idea but I need to fight a battle and win so I can feel in control again. Of course, I may be overreaching in assuming I can win, but that possibility doesn't stop me. It's a short drive to the Shamrock. Funny how bars always have good Irish names. You never see a bar called Stein's or Jones or Antonelli's. I guess long ago Irishmen accepted their gifts, which was an incredible tolerance and enjoyment of beer, and went with it. Maybe my Irish heritage explains some of my problems.

It's the usual dinner crowd. Which is, I can count the total on one hand. I grab my usual place at the end of the bar and order up. Greg is off tonight. Finals coming up, the covering barkeep tells me. Good for him. Hopes he gets out of this place soon. Unexpectedly, I find I kind of miss him though. Strange thing to be attached to the bartender. At the moment it seems rather wise. Better than being attached to someone who actually matters in life. But I have never really seen myself as a stool sitter at the local watering hole sharing life with the barkeep. Turns out I am. And maybe it is where I belong.

The amber liquid is screaming my name. Just one sip, the fire in my throat, would feel so great, so amazing. I swear I see the face of the devil form in the ice in the glass. Maybe this was a bad idea. Maybe I've overestimated myself this time. I lift the glass. Sniff the sickly sweet but pungent odor. My brain is roaring, every neuron yelling, "Do it."

156

My lips touch the cool smooth rim of the glass. I pause, wrestling the demon that runs rampant in my brain. I want this more than anything in the world at this moment. Only I can't. To give in, to lose the battle is to lose everything I have fought for over the last years. I have lost so much over the last few days. But to lose this battle is to lose myself. That's not such a big loss, but I would also lose Bode. I promised him. I swore to him I would never drink again. I couldn't let him down. Not this time.

I put the glass down harshly, with a clunk on the heavy wooden bar. The whiskey splashes out onto my hand. My desperate brain, sensing the losing battle, screams to lick it off my hand. I don't. I wipe my hand on the bar napkin. Sliding off the bar stool, I leave a five dollar bill on the bar and head out, back to the dirty festering wound that is my life.

Chapter 35

I had parked in a little gravel lot around the block from the bar. It is a pretty rundown part of town so it is never crowded even on a good day. Now it is even more deserted. Even with a few decent restaurants nearby, nearly everyone has arrived at their destination restaurant for dinner, or headed home after the early bird special. There is a 1980's Camaro parked next to the driver's side of my Jeep. I roll my eyes. Adult rednecks living in their old teen glory days.

The door swings open as I cross behind it, headed over to my vehicle. I stop short as Joe, the boneheaded guy from my fight at the Shamrock steps out. He looks pissed already and now startled to see me.

I can't exactly pretend I don't see him. I actually consider it for a moment but I am standing five feet from the back of his car. We lock eyes as we both recognize the potential in the encounter.

A thought flashes through my mind. Really? What the hell else could go wrong?

What do I say to someone who knocked me out just last week? After I had inserted myself into his business, justified as I was. Hi? Sorry? Thanks? You bastard? None of those seemed appropriate or effective at defusing his quite evident anger, clearly present before he even laid eyes on me.

Instead I elect to just go on about my business, that being just going home. Sometimes if you just ignore the growling dog and show no fear, it backs down. But Joe is not going to let it be that easy. Damn men and their testosterone driven pride.

"Hey bitch. Where you going?"

I finish crossing past the rear end of his car and come to a stop alongside my Jeep's driver's side, fumbling to get my keys out. He comes up behind me. Too late I realize it is a bad tactical move on my part as I am now cornered between our two vehicles and the cement wall that is the back of the shops on the next street over. Really? Again? Now, after all that has gone on, I have to deal with this asshole?

I turn towards him so as not to be blindsided. Lacking any other witty thing to say, I say just what had come to my mind, "Really? Again?"

"We have unfinished business, you and me."

God, when will people give up on the dumb Hollywood clichés?

"Look man, we're cool. I really don't want to have to do this." I figure if maintain a posture like I could kick his ass maybe he would back down. He's not buying it. I can't say I am surprised but it was worth a shot.

Closing the space between us, he bumps up against mine, his face glaring down into mine. Nasty teeth. The guy has apparently never invested in toothpaste. Or maybe his business involves using methamphetamine. I step back to maintain my space and to escape his foul breath.

"Look. I'm sorry I messed in your business." I almost choke on the apology, but after the last couple of weeks, pragmatic reason is winning over rash impulses. Truth is I am only sorry that I had gotten knocked out and hadn't finished what I had started.

Contrition doesn't work. He doesn't move. I quickly move on to the next plan. Humor.

"Camaro Z28, 1984. Come on. At least go with the classic. A 1968, 69, would make you seem way cooler. This just makes people think you'll pop out with a mullet and a Member's Only jacket."

He cocks his arm as if to punch me. I thought it was funny. Guess he doesn't appreciate my humor.

I consider trying to make it into my Jeep, but the door is locked and he has me backed up enough that I'd have to move him to get the door open. I'm running out of options.

Joe steps back, producing a KA-BAR knife out of his boot. Great, a knife. A big one. Seven inch blade. That thing can do serious and painful damage. I've seen its effect first hand. It's not pretty. It's more of a slow death. Just bleeding out slowly or suffocating from the collapsed lung and tension pneumothorax. Even a slice across the carotids leaves the victim a minute as her blood pools all around her to flash back through her life. I wasn't ready to relive my life, pitiful as it has been, in a moment.

I take another step back, sizing up my escape options, which are pretty much none. If there were no weapons involved, I'm pretty sure I could at least cripple him enough to get past him. But with the knife, my confidence in success is not so much.

The sudden squeal of tires breaks the moment. A minivan with tinted windows screeches to a halt behind us, blocking in both of our vehicles and us with them.

"What the fuck?" Joe spins around just as the side door of the minivan slides open. My brain makes a screaming U-turn in thoughts as the troll pops out, gun drawn. Two quick pops and Joe crumples to the ground in a heap. I watch him fall, as if in slow motion and then look up to see the Glock, complete with silencer pointing dead at my forehead.

The troll breaks into a grin. "I saved your life, Doc. You're my slave for life now."

160

I fail to see the humor in it and just stand there dumbfounded and speechless. My brain scrambles to make sense of what is happening.

Clean Cut calls out of the van from his place in the driver's seat. "Let's go."

The troll grabs my arms and roughly drags me towards the van. I stumble over the lifeless heap of Joe on the ground and nearly fall headfirst into the back of the van. I clamber to right myself, ending up half sitting in the rear bucket seat behind the driver in the process.

Clean Cut's face beams at me as he turns to look at me from the front seat.

"Hi ya, Doc. Good to see you again." With that the troll climbs in next to me and slams the side door shut. Clean Cut calmly pulls out of the parking lot and turns at the next block headed for God only knows where.

Chapter 36

There comes a time, when despite the strongest of resolve, bravado fails. The stiff upper lip starts to quiver. I am at that moment. Seeing a man, even one who was about do slice and dice all over me, shot to death standing right in front of me is shocking.

Sure, I see gunshot wounds all the time. I can no longer count the number of times I've cut someone open, tracing the path of destruction as a hollow point bullet rips its way through soft flesh and hard bone. It has become a scientific exercise. A removed curiosity focused on body parts, only theoretically related to a real life person. It sounds cold and heartless. But it is how you function as a trauma surgeon. If you stop to think about how you hold someone's life in your hands, how every move of the finger can bring death or otherwise destroy a life, you are paralyzed. The weight of the responsibility is too great to really stop and think about, except in quiet moments away from the job when it all overwhelms.

But witnessing the actual real time effect of a bullet on a man has left me shaken. Not to mention the presence of these two bastards in front of me. Not only did I hope and not expect to ever see them again in my life, I certainly had never envisioned being at their mercy once again. My brain is struggling to keep up with the rapidly changing circumstances that have become my life. Once again, control over my own life, my own person, has vanished. And so my bravado is failing. But I can't let them see that.

I sit motionless and speechless, looking out the windows as the houses and trees and other cars rush by. We are headed out to the suburbs, far from my familiar and comfortable territory. I am unsure if seeing where we are going is a good thing or a bad sign. But then I had seen their faces the first time around and lived to tell, so I am cautiously hopeful. Although at this point, the most I dare hope for is to once again simply live through whatever horrible activities they have planned for me.

They let me sit in my silence for a while. I doubt it is out of consideration for my feelings. More likely that these two Neanderthals have a poor grasp of the English language and therefore are rather inept at conversation.

Thoughts race through my mind. Questions burning about what is going on. Why is this happening again? What do they want from me? I think I have an idea on that one but with each question, my anger starts to rise up, overpowering the fear, at least for the moment. I turn to look at the troll who is eyeing me from the seat next to me, gun casually draped on his leg, finger relaxed off the trigger. He smiles a sickening smile as I meet his gaze.

"What is this about? What do you want? You didn't have to kill that guy."

"What? You'd rather I let him go all psycho on your ass?"

How to answer that without showing some sign of gratitude to a man I feel no sense of gratitude towards? No way that I can find, so I let it pass without comment. Clean Cut glances at me in the rearview mirror. Smile lines seen around his eyes. I'm glad someone is enjoying this little adventure.

"What more do you want from me? I did everything you asked."

Clean Cut answers this time, a coherent answer probably too difficult for the mental midget beside me.

"We need your help again, Dr. McCullough."

"What makes you think I will help you again? I know for a fact that Michele is safely away, out of town with her family."

"We have found that most people have more than one leverage point. Even a lone wolf like yourself."

"What the hell are you talking about?"

"I know you would never do what we ask because of a mere threat to you. Not that you are so brave. More that you are just too damn stubborn to give in."

It is a bit disconcerting how accurately he seems to grasp my personality. He is either very intuitive, which I find hard to believe, or somehow, he has learned a lot about my life and who I am. The latter is even more disconcerting; the possibility that this is not some random bad luck on my part. A mental image of my brother and Samson huddling in the prison yard together drifts into my consciousness and makes my stomach drop like a fifty-foot drop on a roller coaster.

My silence seems to give him permission to go on.

"Mr. Davis is quite ill. Seems you were telling the truth about the infection setting in."

Somehow, I find no sense of triumph in being right on this one.

"So now we need you to fix him so he can complete the task that we broke him out to do."

"And what task would that be?" Curiosity rather than true interest.

"He's a computer geek. One of the best hackers in the country. I'm sure you can figure it out from there. But the poor guy is so sick, he pukes when we sit him up in front of the computer. That just won't do."

"And what am I supposed to do about it? I'm a surgeon. I operate on people. In a hospital." Not entirely true, I can and do manage medical problems all the time. But the part about it being done in a hospital is true.

A little laugh from Clean Cut. Again, his confidence only makes me more apprehensive.

"You're a doctor. I know you can do more than operate. You will just have to be a bit creative working outside the hospital. After you see him, you can figure out how you want to fix him. But fix him is exactly what you are going to do."

"Tell me again why I should do anything for you?"

The houses are thinning out now as we have passed through most of the suburbs. Not exactly rural but not exactly houses on top of each other, either. They could shoot me somewhere in the woods out here, and no one would find my body for years. The thought brings a wave of nausea and a taste of bile in my throat. Wish I had gone ahead and had that drink earlier.

Clean Cut slips a hand into his breast pocket and slips out a piece of paper, a photograph. He holds it back over his shoulder for me to see. I take it hesitantly. An overwhelming urge to vomit rolls through my brain and body like a freight train. It is a picture of Bode and me during my visit to see him in prison last week.

Chapter 37

I sit speechless. I don't know if it is from the fear of puking if I open my mouth or the fact that I actually can't put together a complete thought. Fragments of questions and fears and anger bounce around my brain like ping pong balls.

My stupor is broken as we turn off the road onto a gravel driveway. It leads to a house winding down a quarter mile off the road, with a thick patch of trees encircling the house. There is a foreclosure sign in the yard. The house appears to be only a few years old. A large brick structure that looks like any house you would find in a thousand suburban neighborhoods around the country. The landscape had been beautiful at one point but has turned untidy and unkempt. It had been a very nice home for someone until recently.

I hand the photo back to Clean Cut as he pulls to a stop in front of the garage. "How did you get this picture?"

"My boss can get to anyone at any time. That is all you need to know."

"Your boss? So I was right in thinking you're not the brains of the operation."

He smiles slyly, ignoring the thinly veiled insult. He hits a button on the visor and the garage door folds upward. As it reaches its full height, Clean Cut pulls the van into the empty garage. My hopes sink down further as the garage door slides back down into place.

The troll slides open the side door of the minivan and steps out. He leans back in, gun now pointed squarely at my chest and grabs my arm, pulling me out of my seat. A reflexive desire to fight him, to not go easily rises up. I push it aside. It will do no good at this moment and only serve to give him an excuse to be more aggressive. Clean Cut is in charge, but I don't have complete confidence that he can control the situation. This short, mentally challenged, hotheaded, angry guy with a gun in his hand is volatile no matter who is here.

I scoot out of the van, my legs feeling like jelly as my knees threaten to buckle. I need to get it together, find that vein of anger and confidence that can give me some sense of control. At least control over my own reactions to these two assholes. It is the only control I can have at the moment, and I'll be damned if I let them take it away. I clear my throat and stand up a little taller as Clean Cut comes around the van.

The troll opens the solid wooden door that clearly leads to the house and pulls me through by my arm. I shake his grip off.

"I get it. You don't have to manhandle me."

The troll takes a step inches from me. Rubs his body up against my side. A twisted grin on his face.

"Can't help it, Doc. I like touching you."

"Cut it out." Clean Cut steps through separating the two of us. This guy is going to be a real problem. I just pray I am not left alone with him. I'll fight like hell against him, but the gun really guarantees who will win in the end.

"This way, Doc." Clean Cut steps through the mudroom and out into an expansive and expensive kitchen. It is bare, without any of the knickknacks and countertop clutter that make a home.

"Little sparse on the décor. You could do better." I go to my standby. Sarcasm helps me focus. And what I need right now more than anything is focus. That and getting the hell away from here. But that is not happening at the moment. Even if I got away from them, we are in the middle of nowhere, and my bet is they would catch up before I made it to the next house over, as by my guess, it has to be at least a half mile through the woods.

Clean Cut seems amused by me but doesn't let it deter him from the business at hand.

He gestures down a long hallway that leads off the foyer which is at the other end of the kitchen from where we entered. There is an empty great room off to the left. An expansive kitchen island separates the space. Our voices echo in the cavernous space with the granite counter tops and the tile and golden oak flooring. "He's down here."

I head down the hallway, looking in each empty room as I go by. Clean Cut is right on my heels. I pass one room that is full of computer equipment spread on a makeshift table. Plywood resting on sawhorses. Cords weave a tangled web hooking all of the various parts of equipment together. The blinds are pulled down creating a tomb like effect.

Through the next door I find Davis. It is an empty room, someone's bedroom until not too long ago. Davis is curled up on his side on top of a sleeping bag. A balled-up blanket serves as his pillow. He looks like hell. Pale and sweaty. The yellow glow of the overhead light makes him look ghostly. A shell of the guy I broke out just a few nights ago.

My doctor's instincts kick in, and all the fear recedes to the background. Crossing the room, I kneel next to him and gently touch his shoulder. He opens his eyes and gives a weak smile. He seems grateful for the touch or maybe it is just the fact I am here and might be able to help him. Normally I would feel good about having that effect. Right now I don't give a damn how he feels about me.

"Hey Davis. How are you doing?"

"Had better days, Doc."

"Yeah, me too. Let me take a look at your wound."

He gingerly rolls over onto his back, clearly in pain with even this little movement. I tug on the bottom edge of his T-shirt, which is stained with dried bloody fluid, pulling it upwards to get a look at his abdomen.

The wound is angry red, the redness extending several inches in either direction from the wound. The staples are sunken down, the skin swollen causing the staples to lie tightly against the skin. At the top edge, the edges of the wound gape open, and I can see some pus collecting in the open space. It looks bad. But I can't say that. These men need to believe I can fix this. I'm not sure I can. Not here. With nothing to work with.

There is a half empty box of gauze and a roll of tape lying nearby. An almost empty bottle of rubbing alcohol. Their poor attempt at taking care of the wound. I'm not sure I can do much better.

I turn to Clean Cut who is hovering over my shoulder. "Do you have a pen or something similar in shape?" He variously seemed intrigued and ready to hurl at the sight of the wound.

He pulls a roller ball click pen out of his pocket and holds it out for me. Not the best, but it will have to do. I pick up the bottle of alcohol. Drinking it is a sarcastic thought that shoots through my mind. I pour some over the pen and let it drip off the bottom as I hold the top end. I shake off the excess and put down the bottle.

"This is gonna hurt like hell, but I have to probe the wound. I need to know if the fascia is intact." I normally would explain that the fascia is the fibrous, strong tissue that encloses the abdominal cavity, but I don't feel much like having good bedside manner.

Davis grimaces even before I touch him. Just the anticipation seems to cause him pain. I briefly feel sorry for him. I don't like causing pain, even to an asshole like this, I guess.

With my left hand I gently separate the top edges of the wound where the pus has collected. Gloves would be nice, but clearly not an option. Hope to hell the guy doesn't have HIV or Hepatitis C. With my right hand I gently lower the tip of the pen straight down into the wound.

Davis bears down fighting against what must be intense, agonizing pain. The end of the pen disappears into the wound. I slowly lower it further, gently feeling for a floor, a stop point that indicates the fascia is still intact. I pray that it is. If it's not, I doubt I can save this guy in a house in the middle of nowhere. If it is intact, then it is all a superficial wound infection, not peritonitis. That I may be able to get him through. But only if I can get my hands on some antibiotics.

But I am getting ahead of myself. I focus back on my task at hand. I decide to hell with being careful, I plunge my index finger into the wound alongside the pen. I need to feel what is under this. Feel is the surgeon's tool. I ignore the groaning from Davis. Clean Cut has given up his spectatorship and has retreated to the doorway.

My heart skips a beat as I hit the tense firm bottom of the wound. I can feel one of the sutures that holds closed the incision that I had made in the fascia at the original surgery. The edges have already started knitting themselves together, and I can feel no gaps in the incision. No opening into the abdominal cavity.

I pull my finger and the pen out. Davis relaxes a bit. His pain now back to the usually throbbing ache rather than like someone was poking a finger in his wound. I grab some gauze and wipe off my hands. Hopefully they at least have some soap in this place.

I turn to face Clean Cut, who now looks at me expectantly. For a moment, it feels like I am in control of the whole situation. I remind myself that feelings are often wrong. This one sure as hell is.

"I need some sterile saline and a whole lot more sterile gauze. I can wash the wound out and at least get it clean. But it won't matter if he doesn't get some intravenous antibiotics. He needs to be in a hospital."

"That's out of the question, Doc. You know that."

"I can't do anything for him out here in the middle of fucking nowhere." Now I am getting a bit angry. How can they hold me responsible for saving this guy when I can't? No matter how much I want to. To protect Bode. Which, despite all my confusion, I have to assume that is what I am doing. It is an easier place to be in my mind; I am working to protect Bode. Not that Bode has knowingly put me at the mercy of these lunatics. That is a place I just can't go to in my brain, definitely not now and probably not ever.

I stand up, reflexively wiping my hands on my jeans. I can feel the dried stickiness of the pus and blood on my hands. They have to at least have running water here. There clearly is electricity, so a well should be working.

"Look, it doesn't matter what I do here if I don't get him some antibiotics. Strong ones. Not something we can pick up at the local Walgreens."

"Then think, Doc. You are a problem solver. Solve this problem. How can you get your hands on what you need?"

"Well I can't exactly waltz into the hospital with you shoving a gun in my side and ask for them."

He smiles that smirky smile. It's starting to piss me off more than anything.

"You don't need me to go in with you. I trust you, Doc. I know you'll come back. It's who you are. You protect the ones you love at all costs."

He's right on this, again. Even if I was able to tell someone at the hospital what was happening, there is no guarantee the cops could or would get to Bode and protect him in time. I was their prisoner even as I could walk around freely. I couldn't risk anything happening to Bode.

Once I gave them what they wanted last time, I was freed and the threat went away. I could only hope that is would be the same this time around. Until the next time they need something from me. I wipe that last thought away as being completely unhelpful to the situation.

"I need to wash my hands." Mostly I need a few minutes to come up with a plan, without Clean Cut's menacing stare or the troll's grimy hands on me. Clean Cut steps back and points to the end of the hall.

"Bathroom is that way."

I slip past him and take the few short steps to the bathroom. I hesitate for a moment but then shut the door. I am totally in their control whether in sight or not. Clean Cut knows it. I know it. The solitude is welcome. I let out a large exhalation. It feels like the first breath I have taken since I was dragged into the minivan. How long ago was that? It feels like days. Does anyone even miss me? Doubtful. That's the thing with being a loner. No one notices when you don't come home at night. No one will notice until I don't show up for work tomorrow.

I wash my hands thoroughly, thankful that despite being assholes, the guys at least have decent hygiene as evidenced by the hand soap and toothbrushes in the bathroom. A roll of paper towels sits precipitously on the corner of the sink. I splash some water on my face and blot it dry. Staring into my own eyes in the mirror seems suddenly foreign. Like I am looking into someone else's eyes. Like I am living someone else's life.

"Whoever you are, you better think. You need a plan."

Somehow feeling like an outside observer, a spectator, of the events lets my brain relax enough to think through the problem. How to get a hold of IV antibiotics and the equipment needed to start an IV? An idea slowly grows in my brain, finally giving birth to a plan. I know how to do it.

Chapter 38

There was no way around my needing to go to the hospital to obtain
what was needed. After a brief conversation with Clean Cut regarding
this matter, he had agreed. Thus I'm cruising back into the city with
the troll behind the wheel. We set out early to get there before it gets
too busy and crowded. Clean Cut has gone to obtain the dressings and
saline, both items of considerable bulk and easily obtainable at a
pharmacy. No need for my lugging a huge bagful of stuff out. The
more discrete the better.

Clean Cut has also asked, actually more like demanded, that I
quickly obtain everything I needed in this one trip and then come up
with a reason why I would be away from the hospital for the next few
days. Seems his trust in his leverage over me only goes so far. He's
worried that the more I'm out of his sight and in my own element, the
more likely I will be to try to get word to Bode and make a break for
it for myself. I can't say I disagree with him.

We pull into the parking garage and the troll glides the
minivan into an open spot near the entrance walkway to the hospital.
He throws it into park as my hand reaches for the door handle. He
grabs my arm, freezing me in place. I look down at his hand, quite
tired of his groping me at every chance. Then straight in his eyes.
There's no smile, no look of amusement. He is all business, and his
left hand on the butt of the Glock tucked in his waistband just serves
to prove the point.

"You get in and you get out. No fucking around. No tipping
anyone off. No trying to make a break for it."

I tug my arm away. "Yeah, I got it. Relax."

I pop the door open and slide out. "Besides, until I know Bode is safe, I am not going to fuck with you guys. Okay." As soon as I said it, I regret it. No need to share any sexually charged words with this asshole.

The troll slides out and catches up with me at the entrance to the walkway.

"I'll just wait in the lobby for you. Okay? No shit. I mean it."

"Suit yourself. It is going to take twenty or thirty minutes so don't freak out, okay?"

By this point we have crossed the walkway bridge to the hospital entrance. The soaring rooflines highlight an expansive lobby tastefully arranged with the latest contemporary and uncomfortable furniture. You would think comfort would be the guiding principle in decorating a hospital where anxious and scared people wait for hours on end to find out the fate of their loved ones. Nope, it is all about style and flash.

The early morning sun shines through the sky lights, creating a warm and enveloping golden glow. I actually take a breath to enjoy it. Having spent the night locked in that house with men who could end my life at any moment has made me more appreciative of a new day.

The troll breaks off, with a nod for emphasis, and goes to find a seat. I turn right and follow the hallway to the main part of the hospital.

Just like the rest of the world today, hospital systems have kept up with the digital age. We have all computerized systems, including charting and order entry. A doctor logs into a computer anywhere in the hospital and can enter orders for any patient located at any place in the hospital. The order then is spit out in the appropriate place for the person who has to complete the order. Nursing orders pop out at the nurses' stations and on their computers.

175

Radiology orders pop up down in the radiology department.
Medication orders pop up in the pharmacy.

But for all the high tech digital sophistication, there are some
things that are old-fashioned analog systems. Such is the pneumatic
tube system. Medications cannot be digitally sent to the location in
the hospital where it is needed. Medicines used frequently are stocked
on each nursing unit. And patients who are receiving the same
medicines on a scheduled basis get their own little drawer in a
medicine cart on each unit. Those medicines are delivered by a
pharmacy tech once or twice a day.

New medicines, or one time medicines, however, are often
sent through the pneumatic tube system. Yup, just like the kind you
see at a bank drive thru. Only this system is a spider web of tubes
with dozens of stations where things can be sent and received. It is no
surprise that such a web, with large plastic containers shooting along
at high speed, often gets jammed or stopped off. More than once, a
urine specimen, with a not fully tightened lid, has made a mess of the
tube system. It is a regular occurrence for the system to go down and
not be usable.

I need the pneumatic system not to work in order for my plan
to work. But I am not so optimistic to think that it will suddenly crash
right now when I need it to. Somehow, I don't think the fates, if any
exist, are smiling kindly on my current activities. No, I need to crash
the system intentionally, right now.

I have given this a lot of thought on the drive in. In all
honestly, I don't really know what causes the crashes all the time.
Other than the flying piss. I think I have come up with what seems
like a high probability way to jam it up. I walk by several nursing
units, giving the usual hellos and heys to everyone. I finally find one
that is relatively deserted. On my ways through the halls, I snag a
stethoscope off an isolation cart. Patients with resistant bacteria get an

isolation cart with gowns and gloves for the medical staff to wear when working with the patient. A stethoscope is included that is exclusively used for that patient. Not the best quality. Seems more like it came from a Fisher Price doctor play kit. But that's beside the point.

It is the perfect thing to jam up the tube system. At the mostly deserted nursing station, I step up to the tube system panel. Slipping the stethoscope out of my bag, I flip open a heavy plastic container that acts as the carrier. Carefully positioning the stethoscope in the container, I make sure the bell of the scope is hanging out. It takes a little force to still get the container latched, but for once, I am glad for the cheap quality of the stethoscope. The tubing smashes down easily. I slip the carrier into the ready position and pick a random destination. The OR sounds good. I type in the appropriate code of that location, press send and say a prayer.

The machine cranks to life and starts to slide the carrier into position. As I hold my breath, a sudden whoosh comes and the carrier is gone. I hear the clunking fading away into the ceiling. First step down.

As I wait for the system to come to a grinding halt, jammed up by the poorly packaged carrier, I head off to get the first of the supplies that I need. Davis needs intravenous antibiotics, which means I need to get my hands on the supplies to start an IV. I elect to not try to get any IV fluids. Too heavy and bulky to get out in my slender messenger bag.

The supplies are locked up in the supply room on each nursing unit. Literally, you can't get a band-aid or a Tylenol in the hospital without getting into some locked and restricted place. If a staff member gets a headache, he or she better have a personal stash of Ibuprofen or clock out for a trip to the convenience store. Ironic, I know.

Fortunately, security is not exactly designed like a bank vault. The supply rooms have a numerical keypad. The combination is more often than not, the four-digit phone extension of the nursing unit. This is not information someone will offer up to you, but over time, it's not hard to figure out.

Again, I manage to find a relatively quiet unit. All the nurses are busily tending to their patients. It is early morning and the new shift has much to do to get their day off right. No one notices as I slip into the supply room. It is a wall-to-wall, floor-to-ceiling shelf of medical supplies – dressings, tapes, tubing, drains, etc. I run my hand along the shelves, looking for what I need. About half way down, I find it - IV angiocaths with tubing, stopcocks and extension tubing. I grab a couple of each. Why go to all of this trouble just to find I grabbed the only defective one in the bunch?

I slip these into my bag just as the overhead loud speaker's squeaks to life. "Attention hospital personnel – the pneumatic tube system is down. The pneumatic tube system is down."

It isn't exactly a moment of excitement I feel. Or even satisfaction. I think it is more relief. On to the next step. I slip out of the supply room and head over to the surgical unit. Fortunately my patient who was hit by the car is still in the hospital. I can order an antibiotic without raising any red flags in the pharmacy.

I log onto a computer in the physician work area. Again, some small talk with the people I know so well. Yet I feel as though I am in a completely different world at the moment. As if I am sleep walking, just going through the motions. Thankfully, no one really notices my distracted demeanor.

I click on Mr. Kutchen's account and then on the order entry tab. Up pops the order window. I type in Meropenem. It's a powerful antibiotic but at the moment I am less concerned with causing resistant bacteria than I am with having to treat one. I'd rather err on the side of more than needed than not powerful enough. I go through the usual steps of dose and time selection. For duration I type in three doses. Hopefully, the pharmacy will release all three doses at once. It's a gamble but I don't know any way around it. I may have to sweet talk someone downstairs to ensure I get all three. With one more click, the order is placed.

The last step is going to be the trickiest. It involves some fast-talking on my part and interaction with staff, all while trying not to raise any suspicions. I take a deep breath, check my watch and head downstairs to the basement where the pharmacy is located. It has been twenty minutes since I left the troll down in the lobby. I can only hope he is not freaking out.

On the walk downstairs, I give consideration to my options at this point. I could just walk out of the hospital on the backside and disappear. Saves me but doesn't help Bode as I am sure if I'm not back downstairs in the lobby in the next five or ten minutes, a phone call will be made. Or I could try to alert someone here at the hospital as to what is going on.

The problem with that is that I am a loner. Michele is my best friend and knows me well, my secrets, my history. As for the rest of the people I work with day in and day out, they just know me as a friendly, competent and work-driven surgeon. No more than that. All I share is casual greetings and vague personal information. So to have to explain everything to someone in a timely fashion so that it makes sense and is believable just seems like a long shot at the moment. Not a risk I am willing to take with Bode's life.

I can only hope my opportunity will come somewhere along the line. As long as Davis is alive but still sick, I have time to figure out something. So I will wait. Hopefully I can come up with something before I am no longer needed by the evil trio.

Coming to the pharmacy door, I knock lightly. Wait a moment. Knock a little harder. It has a numerical keypad, of course. This code I don't know. But the door swings open finally. Darla, a pharmacy tech I vaguely recognize from passing her in the hallways, swings it wide and then scoots back to the bench where she is labeling medicines. I slip through the door, letting it swing shut behind me. Better to not have someone come up behind me. I am so on edge I think my head would explode.

"Hi, Dr. McCullough. What are you doing down in these parts?"

That is the effect of being the only female trauma surgeon in the system. There are scores of staff members I only know by sight as being someone who works here, while everyone knows who I am.

"Hi, umm."

She graciously saves me. "Darla."

I smile warmly. "Of course, I'm sorry. I am so bad with names."

She smiles back, a genuine warm comfortable smile.

"What can I do for you?"

"Well, as you know, the tube system is down. Big surprise there. But I need some antibiotics stat for my patient. I figured I would just come down and get them."

"Oh yeah, that must be the ones I am just labeling right now. You caught me without any other stat orders so I could process it right away."

"Do you have all three ready?"

"Just labeling the last one; do you need all three at once?"

"I just figured I'd take them all in one trip. I'll put them in Kutchen's drawer in the med cart. That way it will all be taken care of. I know he's gonna need them."

Darla's smile fades and she looks a bit unsettled. This is not the usual protocol. I find myself holding my breath. Please let this work. Please.

The smile returns, and I let out a big exhalation.

"Sure, why not? Thanks for coming down so we don't have to run it up there."

She stacks up the three plastic bags of liquid medicine and hands them to me. I fight the urge to shove them in my bag and run. Instead I bundle them in the crook of one arm as I pull the door open with my free hand. Just one more moment and I'll be home free.

"Dr. McCullough?"

Shit, please don't let her get suspicious now. I am so close.

I look back over my shoulder and give a painted on smile. "Yes?"

"I just wanted to say thank you. You operated on my grandma last year, and she came through it beautifully. You did a great job."

I almost drop the medicines as the tautness of my muscles release at her comment.

"You're welcome. I'm glad she did so well."

With that I scoot out of the door into the hallway. After taking a moment to shove the medicine bags into my messenger bag, piling them on top of the other stolen supplies, I make a beeline for the lobby.

Halfway there, I remember my deal with Clean Cut to explain my absence for several days. I can't use my cell as that was taken away last night. Instead I stop by one of the internal hospital phones. I punch in several numbers and wait for the ring. I really hope I get the machine and not a person. No such luck.

"Surgical services, this is Karen."

"Karen, it's Dr. McCullough."

"Oh honey, how are you holding up? I haven't seen you since all that craziness with the prisoner escaping. You okay?"

At least she gives me the opening I need.

"That's just it. I've been trying but I think I need to get away for a few days. I don't have any cases posted, and the guys offered to cover my call this week in light of everything."

"That's surprising."

"What? I'm sorry, I just really need some time away."

"No honey, not that. The fact that those testosterone filled surgeons would be so thoughtful as to cover for you without me brow beating them into it."

I laugh weakly. "Yeah, go figure. So can you all live without me for a bit?"

"Absolutely. But only for a bit, hon. We'll miss you. Just call me when you have an idea when you'll be back."

"That's sort of up in the air. Some unexpected things going on. But I promise to call you as soon as I get an idea."

With that I hang up and nearly run to the lobby. The tension of sneaking around in broad daylight among people who trust me is about ready to overwhelm me. Getting out of this place is all I can think about. Even if it means going back to that cursed house.

Chapter 39

It is a long and silent ride back to the prison house. Needless to say, I don't really feel like making small talk with the troll. I suspect he is just learning mastery of two syllable words anyway. Instead I occupy my mind thinking about all kinds of random and somewhat unimportant questions.

Like wondering about how long before the nurse realizes that the medicine ordered hasn't come up from the pharmacy. And what the pharmacist will think about my absconding with an antibiotic. Dilaudid, Morphine, Demerol, the strong narcotics, yes, that makes sense. Meropenem? All I can imagine is a great big "Huh?"

Eventually I will have to go back and face the consequences of my actions. If I make it back. It is this thought that brings my brain back to things that actually matter at this moment. Like how the hell I am going to get out of this situation? How am I going to protect Bode in that process? More and more I can't help thinking that the end of this is not going to go in my favor if it is not in my control. Letting me live once was lucky, expecting them to let me live a second time is just down right unlikely. So I busy myself trying to come up with another plan. This one for my benefit only. Not for the asshole dying back at the house.

With that, we pull in the driveway. Clean Cut is already back and waiting for us as we walk back into the house. Edgy and annoyed would be a fair appraisal of his mood.

"You were gone a while. Better have the stuff you need."

I drop my bag on the counter as an answer. He takes a peek in and briefly rifles through it as if he knows what he is looking at.

"I got the supplies you asked for from the pharmacy. Went to several actually, so no one wondered about my buying out the entire supply in one place."

I decide to try out my own smirk as I reply paired with the deepest sarcasm I can muster. "Oh, aren't you clever." In return I just get that same damn smirking smile.

He throws my bag at me and points down the hallway. "Go to work, Doc."

I move slowly, looking into each room again, desperately seeking something that can give me an advantage. All of them are empty except the computer room and the one Davis is occupying. The only possibility is all of the computer equipment in the spare room. Somehow I can't imagine them letting me send out some emails in my spare time. Maybe I can bash each of them over the head with the CPU. An internal snort at that ridiculous thought.

Davis looks like crap. He is still laid out on the sleeping bag. Sweating profusely and shivering all at the same time. There is no way that only three doses of antibiotics are going to be enough. But that is not information I am about to share. What I have is the best I could hope for. There was no way I could have gotten more without setting off all kinds of alarms. The lack of a true cure just makes the need for a plan all the more pressing. All I am buying with the treatment is a little time. I have a day, maybe two at most, to get the hell out of here.

But for now I am going to stick to the rules. Human nature is to acclimate to a situation and to let one's guard down. I am not acclimating to being held prisoner and doing someone else's bidding. But I am hoping the shmucks will get used to having me around. If they think I am not going to be trouble, then maybe they will let their guard down and I will have an opening to be just that.

Davis groans as I loosen the dressing I had placed over his wound. It is still angry red and the pus I had cleaned out has already re-accumulated.

"Sorry. This is going to hurt. I have nothing to give you for that."

Stealing antibiotics was easy compared to all of the red flags trying to make off with narcotics would have raised. And truth is I don't really care if the guy is in pain. Not exactly living up to the Hippocratic Oath, I know, but I am pretty sure Hippocrates never dealt with a situation like this. Besides, pain never killed anyone so in truth, I am not doing harm.

Clean Cut drops his bag of supplies next to me and then retreats out of the room. Typical tough guy with no stomach for anything real. How many times have I seen the macho guy hit the floor as soon as the blood starts to flow?

Davis grimaces in anticipation. I sort through the supplies from the Clean Cut's bag. Several packages of four by four gauze, a roll of medical grade tape, several large bottles of saline and a staple remover. Clean Cut had stared at me in horror when I told him to get that. How the hell did he think the staples come out of a wound? In the hospital we have fancy looking expensive equipment for it but it is really just a glorified staple puller.

First I grab the staple remover. I need to remove the top couple of staples so all of the pus can be washed out. With the skin edges open, the wound will eventually close in from the deeper portion up. That is, if he lives long enough. Davis grunts as I pull the top three staples out. Just like pulling a staple out of paper. Fortunately, the lower half of the wound seems to be healing pretty well. Maybe he'll make it. But I'm not betting my life on that fact.

Next, I grab a bloody shirt that is in the corner. It's dried now so will work fine to soak up all the saline I am about to pour out.

"Roll up on your side a bit."

Davis obliges as I stuff the shirt as a wedge in the corner where his side meets the floor, directly below the wound. Taking the bottles of saline, I poke a hole in the top of each bottle. One by one I aim the make shift nozzle at the wound. Opening it slightly with my fingers, I am able to get a good stream washing into the wound. It pours down onto the shirt, soaking it an instant. The blood and pus wash away, and the draining stream starts to run clearer. After three bottles, I think it is the best I am going to get under these circumstances.

I have to give credit to Davis. He turns pale and looks as though he is about to puke, but he never utters a word. I had expected a stream of expletives throughout the process.

"That's it. I'm done."

He rolls back onto his back and lets out a big sigh. Taking the gauze Clean Cut had bought, I soak a couple of pieces with saline and stuff it into the open area of the wound. Then I take another piece of four by four gauze and tape it in place over the packing.

"We'll have to change this twice a day until it starts to close in."

"How long will that take?"

I meet his questioning gaze with my own. For a moment I see him only as one of my patients and forget the circumstances under which it is such. He's so young and fragile looking. I almost feel sorry for him. Almost.

"A while." That's the best hope I could offer him at this moment. "I need to start an IV so we can get this antibiotic into you."

"Okay." He offers up his arm willingly. Damn it. I can't afford to start caring about this guy beyond what I am forced to worry about.

Truth is, there is a good chance I can't fix him. I can slow things down, give him a fighting chance. But he needs to be in a hospital with medicines and professional wound care.

Getting the IV started is a bit challenging as he is so dehydrated from his infection that his veins are pretty flat. Clearly he has not been eating and drinking much. But he's young enough that the vein walls are hardy and the vein doesn't blow as I get a good return of blood and then flush with saline. I deftly tighten the lock of the extension tubing to the IV catheter and snugly tape the whole thing in place. I have a spare, but if he knocks this one out just moving around, it'll leave us with nothing else if a second one fails.

I pull one of the bags of medicine out of the bag and spike it with the other end of the IV tubing. The room is basically empty, so there is nothing really to hang it from. Looks like I will just have to stand and hold it. Hopefully, I can just run it in and not scorch his vein. I confess, the particulars of medicine administration is not something I pay much attention to at work. I order it. The nurses know how to give it.

Davis isn't screaming about burning veins so I take that as a good sign. I gently squeeze the bag, encouraging the flow rate. It only takes a few minutes before the bag is empty.

I wish I could look at the wound and see it clearing up in the instant I give the meds. But things don't work that way, no matter how I wish it at the moment. Time is what it will take. But the great unknown is how much time Davis will take to get either better or much worse. And how much time I have left.

Chapter 40

The rest of the night passes uneventfully. I am designated to sleep in the room with Davis. Locked in, of course. Never mind the windows that I could climb out. But Davis, sick as he is isn't completely out of it and would scream his bloody head off if I make a break for it. Plus I have come up with a plan to get both myself and my brother out of danger. And that plan does not include me making a break for it, yet.

Needless to say, I do not sleep well. I am not sure I truly sleep at all. What little time I spend in slumber is raft with nightmares and thoughts of all the things that could yet go wrong. Not to mention the lingering doubt about Bode's involvement in all of this. And the guilt over my actually considering that possibility. I have known him my whole life, but is it just the Bode I want to see, an image I have crafted of him in my head to make me feel better? He lied about Dad. What else could he be lying about? If he thinks he belongs in prison, did he decide to become the kind of person who does the types of things that land you in prison?

And what about Mike? To doubt Bode is to give credence to his accusations. And I am too angry, too hurt to allow the possibility that he was right to question. Things are much simpler if I can believe he used me, manipulated me to get information. Hurts like hell but gives clarity rather than confusion. In the endless circling in my brain, the only way I can find to get off the merry go round is to back Bode. Blood trumps lust. To hell with Mike. Except for the fact I need him to make my plan work. But I am not above using someone. Especially one who used me.

I spend the early hours before dawn leaning against the wall, trying to quiet the screaming in my back from the night on the floor, watching my patient sleep quietly. His color looks better. Somewhere between a healthy pink glow and the ashen gray of death. The power of medicines to heal still amazes me at times. I just hope it is powerful enough.

Just as he awakes the doorknob rattles and the door swings open. Clean Cut enters and tosses a MacDonald's bag at me. Not that I am a health nut, but the thought of adding an Egg McMuffin to the acid churning in my stomach is enough to turn me green. I wordlessly let the bag fall at my feet.

"Good morning kids." The smirk.

His sarcastic perkiness makes me want to punch him. I don't. Yet, I think to myself. Okay, maybe I still have not learned my lesson in being selective about who I take on. But just the image of me doing it is enough to bring me a certain sense of satisfaction. Fortunately, that is enough. Even fools can learn.

"Davis, you look much better. Doc, you're a miracle worker."

Davis sits up and makes an effort to stand. A little wobbly but he makes it. "I feel better. Hurt like hell."

I scramble to my feet. I am powerless enough without having them literally towering over me. "You need to take it easy. You are not out of the woods yet."

"Yeah, it's all good. I'll take it slow, but I think I can work a little."

"What kind of work are you doing exactly?" Maybe I am a fool, asking that question. But I figure for all the shit I've been through, I have a right to know.

Davis glances at Clean Cut who just shrugs. Davis takes this as an okay.

"I'm really good with code."

"So you are hacking into computers?"

"Not exactly. Worm building."

"You write computer code to create a worm program?"

"Yup, best around. It will go out to all the major financial institutions and collect information."

"You mean like people's personal information?"

"Yup. Worth huge money on the open market. I get the data, the boss sells it. We all get rich. Well, I get rich. I don't know who the boss is, but I know he is already loaded."

"You don't know who you are working for?" It seems incredulous to me that someone would risk their life for a shadow.

"Nope. Max here is my contact. Don't really care as long as the check clears." He laughs at this, the only one who finds it funny.

I shrug my shoulders and look out the window. I could die because some asshole wants to drive a Lamborghini. The day is going to be clear and bright. I am sure somewhere, someone is excited about the day, looking forward to its unfolding. The branches of a large oak on the edge of the yard sway ever so slightly in the breeze. The small green buds of spring are starting to show, adding a touch of color to the dark of the woods that lies beyond.

Clean Cut turns towards Davis. "I gotta go, be back tomorrow, man. Derek is here to watch her so you can get to work."

Davis grimaces as he takes a few tentative steps. "I'll fire things up and make sure I have everything I need."

I fight the reflex to reach out to steady him. I won't make it easy for any of them. "Take it easy. You're still sick. And I'm still responsible for you."

I feel the approach of Clean Cut behind me. I turn to meet his gaze as Davis totters out the door.

"It's nice to know you still care about your patient, Doc."

"Don't mistake concern for compassion. If he doesn't make it, I don't make it. It's simple self-preservation."

"That's my girl, smart mouth and smart brain. No Davis, no you, no brother."

"Yeah, we covered that. Anything else?"

"Behave yourself. Derek can be a bit... well, let's say temperamental. I can't say what would happen if you start trying to be all clever while I'm gone."

"If he touches me, I'll kick his ass from here to October."

The smirk turns into a grin, equally as creepy. "I'm sure you'd try. Yup, I'm sure you would. Do me and yourself a favor and just stay put in here. Amuse yourself."

"How? By imagining all the ways I'd like to use a scalpel on you without anesthesia?"

He brings his hand up suddenly and grabs my face, squeezing my jaw in his thick strong hands. "Someday that smart mouth is gonna say too much."

He pats me gently on the cheek and turns on his heel to leave. "Leave the door open. I won't be long."

It takes a moment for my pulse rate to come back out of the stratosphere from the sudden physicality. I really need to learn to not speak my mind so freely. My body settles back to the persistent mostly terrified state that has become the norm. But as much as I fear being alone in the house with the troll, I can't help but feel a ray of hope that maybe my opening will come. A whole lot of other stars still need to align, but decreasing the numbers in the house is a start. I can only hope and wait.

Chapter 41

It's not likely Davis will last too long working. Patients tend to do that. They feel better and assume all is cured and jump back into life headlong. The body doesn't usually agree with the mind on that one and makes it known. I suspect within a couple of hours he clearly will be ready to lie down.

By now, I have made my way down to the kitchen. Not that I am seeking the company of the troll, but I am bored out of my head, going a bit stir crazy, and tired of waiting. Crazy ideas of creating my own opportunity, take the offensive, are now running through my head. I fight the urge to act on one of these ideas, knowing I will be destined to fail. And failure was truly not a good option.

I am not looking to make small talk. Rather I lean up against the counter, sipping on a glass of water and looking out the window. I can feel the stare of the troll on me from across the room. I really don't appreciate being undressed, even if just in his imagination. I can't shake the fear that this could all end very badly for me, and it would involve this asshole having what he would deem fun and I would find a nightmare.

Davis toddles in, looking a bit paler than earlier. "I think I overdid it."

"I told you to take it easy. People never listen to their doctors." A lame attempt at humor falls quite flat. There then exists a very long moment of silence as we all size each other up. I nearly drop my glass as the shrill ring of the troll's cell phone startles the silence away.

He checks the caller ID and then clicks to pick up.

"Hey, babe."

I can't help but be curious and a bit taken aback by the thought of this ass having a normal relationship with anyone. But I guess even the most despicable, evil person in the world has a mother who loves him, even if it is in a twisted yet sincere way.

The troll turns his back as the voice spilling out on the other end sounds a loud note of anger.

"No, babe. I told you, it's a business trip. It will still be a few more days."

Davis grins. I am not sure if it is sympathy for the troll or pure amusement that the guy is getting hassled. "Girlfriend. She gives him such shit."

The troll glances over his shoulder and steps towards the door leading out to the patio area. He has turned my life upside down, threatened me, assaulted me and plans God know what else and he's worried about his privacy? I'm still trying to process and picture him in a relationship with a girlfriend. Who would have him? Does she know what his "job" is?

Davis shrugs. "I'm gonna go lay down. I feel like shit."

I stand frozen for a moment as he disappears down the hall. I hear the bedroom door creak as he swings it shut. I can see the troll out on the patio, pacing back and forth. Alternatively listening and then trying to answer the girl on the other end of the line.

This is my moment. The stars are aligned, but only if I get my head out of my ass and move. Placing my glass gently down on the counter, I tiptoe towards the hallway, heading for the computer room. I spy my bag, which had been taken from me and thoroughly ransacked several times in the corner of the kitchen.

I know they took my cell, but I pray Clean Cut didn't pay any attention to the business card buried at the bottom. Mike's business card. With his email address on it. I have no intention of making amends but he is the key to my plan, to Bode's survival. I quickly rifle through the random receipts and scraps of paper pooling in the bottom. A moment of excitement and hope pulse through me as I pull it out.

I glance out the window to be sure the troll is still deep in conversation, mid-reprimand. I hope that chick has a lot to say when she is pissed, because I need a moment. Clearly the idiot cares about her, because he seems to be taking it quietly, clearing being contrite and apologetic.

I slip into the computer room and slip into the chair behind the desk. Several monitors are lined up. I pull the keyboard towards me and wiggle the mouse. One of the screens jumps to life. I click on the programs folders. There has to be an Internet connection in order to send out a worm. I just hope it isn't set up behind some crazy security system. Computers aren't my thing. I can click and type. Email, Internet surfing, PowerPoint and documents. That's about it. And iTunes.

I click on the Google chrome icon. A window pops up, the little circle at the top tab spinning. Come on, come on. Never has an Internet connection seemed so incredibly slow. But in a moment the page loads. I quickly log onto my email account. I consider checking to see where the troll is, but I don't want to waste precious time looking. I press on, risking everything based on some woman I don't know, will never meet and don't care about. I only care that she is a talker.

My email loads quickly. Thirty-four new messages. Ignoring them all, I click on compose. Glancing at the business card I carefully type in the email address neatly printed at the bottom. Better not screw that up; this is the only chance I have. Having it returned for a bad address would be the height of failure.

I quickly type my message, trying to be as succinct as possible. It basically comes down to this – I am in trouble. My brother is in danger. Please go up to the prison and make sure that he is safe from everyone there. I'll be okay.

The last part I am most uncertain of. In fact, I am fearful the whole plan is worthless. I am trusting my brother's life to a man who has proven clearly to have no trust in me. Who accused me of being a part of this whole insanity. Maybe it is a leap of faith, a leap off a very high and very steep cliff. Or it is just an act of desperation. I have no one else who can do this for me. Sometimes life forces us to trust, even when every brain is screaming otherwise.

I click send. The moment it takes to process feels like an hour. "Message sent" pops up. My heart skips a beat as I hear the outside door open. I shove the business card in my jeans pocket and hurry to the doorway. I pop out just as troll comes around the corner. I can only hope he buys my desperate acting as I turn towards the closed door at the end of the hall, pretending to just be walking that way.

"Hey, what the hell are you doing?" With one stride, he is right behind me. Grabbing my arm roughly, he spins me around and pulls me up against himself.

I shake my arm free and step back.

"Get the hell off of me. I'm just going to check on Davis and change his dressing. It's almost time for his next dose of antibiotics."

I turn back and place my hand on the doorknob. I pause a fraction of a second, waiting for a blow to fall or some other act of violence. Instead the troll glares at me for a second and then spins on his heels and goes back to the kitchen.

Chapter 42

It is amazing where the mind will go when you are in the dark, alone and afraid. All kinds of ghosts, real and imagined come out to haunt and torment. This is the place I find myself. I changed Davis' dressing and he has drifted off to sleep. I sit staring out the window, seeing nothing but a world full of doubts and fears.

My leap off of the merry go round of doubt and fear the night before is apparently temporary. As the dark encircles me, the thoughts go round and round. Mike questioning me, doubting me. No, more than that, accusing me. How could he think I would risk my best friend's life, or even put her in a situation so terrifying? My anger is weirdly juxtaposed with the hope that even now he is working to help me, to help Bode.

I circle back to Bode and the unsettling possibility that maybe I do not know him. The events and revelations of the last week are like a brick loosened from the pedestal I have built for him. I have for so long seen him the way I want him to be, the way I need him to be to make things right for myself. But what if all that I believe of him is untrue? If not all, then even some.

I consider the possibility and it causes a queasy sensation in stomach. Bode told me he was friends with Samson. He seemed quite comfortable with the idea of being buddies with a convicted felon. The irony of that thought is mostly lost on me in this moment. Could Bode have set me up? Have used me to help out a buddy? No. No, that cannot be true. That cannot be reality.

Maybe he had no choice. Maybe he had a debt he could not repay in any other way. If that was the case, I would have volunteered. He could have just asked me. I would give my life to protect him. But then was Mike so wrong to suspect me? Or did Bode risk my life to protect his own? Can I blame him after what my actions have cost him?

The questions keep swirling, building into crashing waves that brings tears to my eyes, a silent shudder to my shoulders, a quiver to my lips. Can we ever really know another person? No matter how close, how intimate, don't we all have a secret place, a secret person inside that is known by no one? A person who may be capable of many things unthinkable. The right circumstances. The right influences.

If it is true then I am to blame. My actions on that night years ago have led to all of this. How could it be any other way? The path from there to here was inevitable. This crystallizes like a shining diamond in my mind ignoring the part that screams "No! You are wrong." The brain can be so deceptive, seeing patterns where none exist. Finding cause and effect between distantly related events, skipping over the hundred intervening happenings that led to the road taken. Turning possibilities into fact and impressions into truth. Guilt and blame are clever and won't let facts get in the way. The burden exists, whether it belongs or not.

I shake my head to clear the thoughts. It is too confusing. Too frightening. I need to focus on the immediate task at hand. Escaping from this hell. Over and over, I refocus on this, turning back from the black hole that threatens to consume me, to render me helpless and hopeless. Hours pass as I live suspended in this world of doubt and fear. Without sleep, the night passes by. At some point exhaustions overcomes me. I drift off into a brief, haunted, restless, tormented sleep.

Chapter 43

Awakening, I find Davis has stirred. He sits up staring at me, half at me, half off into a distant world no one else can see. Coming close to death can change a person. I don't know if it has changed this man. My only concern is keeping death from having its way right now.

The grey light of early dawn has settled into the room, throwing deep shadows in the corners. I sit up rubbing my eyes, my face, trying to will some energy. The adrenaline of the past days has burned itself out leaving only exhaustion and discouragement.

I am still debating about when to take my next step towards freedom. How long do I give Mike to get to Bode and protect him? Maybe he isn't even going to help at all. Should I wait, hoping his conscience and curiosity get the best of him? Do I make a move before the third member of this little dysfunctional family comes back? The thoughts circle endlessly without finding an end that makes up a solution.

Davis drags himself up to his feet. His color continues to improve and his strength seems better. He looks less like a frail eighty year old and more like the young vibrant twenty-three year old he is supposed to be.

"How are you feeling?"

"Better. Don't hurt as much. Don't feel like I want to hurl all the time."

"That's good. The drugs are doing the job. There is only one more dose of the IV antibiotics so that's good. You may get by with switching to PO meds soon."

"P.O.?"

"Pills. By mouth."

"Oh, yeah. Medical lingo."

"Well, you have computer-ese. I have medical slang. We all have our own languages."

"I'm going to go do some work while I'm feeling better. I hope Max gets back soon with some food. I'm starving."

"Good sign. Wish I felt like eating."

Davis pauses for a moment at the door. I can almost see a look of sympathy or compassion or concern. "I'm sorry you got caught up in all of this. You have been really nice to me and saved my life. I won't forget that."

"Please don't. Because I am not sure your cohorts feel quite so grateful and indebted."

He shrugs and vanishes. If he is my hope for survival, I am not reassured.

After a few moments I make my way out to the kitchen. The troll is doing nothing in particular. A brief image of what I think is going through his mind - the old-fashioned color bars on the broadcast television channels late at night. Actually, no, I don't give him much credit.

It occurs to me that I should engage in conversation. Somewhere in the back of my mind I recall some wisdom of making your captors see you as a real person by engaging with them. Likely from some 1980's rerun cop show. I consider, although doubt that it is ever terribly effective.

I barely see them as people at this point, and I suspect their view on me is something similar. Although I do confess, the phone call from the girlfriend, wife, significant other, whatever, has given me a new perspective on the troll. But try as I might, I can't imagine someone actually loving this Neanderthal. Call it a lack of imagination, but it seems to be true.

I try to come up with monosyllabic words to start a conversation with. I know, I shouldn't be so judgmental. He could have a PhD for all I know. But my hatred for him requires me to belittle him endlessly, both in my mind and out loud. The latter has not really worked in my best interest, so I am trying to stick with the internal mocking.

Of course, he may very well be passing judgment on me. He thinks of me as an arrogant, self-serving, petulant surgeon with a God complex. A characterization to which I take exception. Anyone who thinks getting out of bed in the dead of winter at four in the morning to go take out a spleen of some dumbass who thought driving his pickup backwards at eighty miles per hour while drunk was a good idea has a strange definition of self-serving. And as far as thinking I am God, I definitely don't think it and I don't want it. It's a job I'll pass on every time. Although I have to say, the idea of smiting someone seems a bit fun at the moment.

Since I am busy having my own internal conversation, the room remains silent. Clearly, the way he wants to know me most is naked as he imagines me in his head every time he looks at me, which he is doing now. I stare back, tired of pretending he is not doing that and tired of being scared of him.

I take a deep breath, clear my throat and attack it like a clinical problem. Sometimes things take brute force, sometimes it takes finesse. I decide to go with the finesse. I can't guarantee any semblance of sincerity but I can at least try to pretend I don't despise this man with every fiber of my being.

"Girlfriend giving you shit?" I have to admit, I sort of want to rub that in.

His mouth opens but nothing comes out. Stops for a moment, clearly uncertain how to proceed with a civil conversation with me. But to his credit, he decides to try to be a human being.

"Yeah. No matter what I do, it's never good enough." He rubs his hand over his prematurely balding head.

"Relationships are a lot of work." I wanted to add "especially when you are an asshole." But I rein in my tongue before it slips out as clearly it would be counterproductive.

"Ain't that the truth? She's great. I love her and all but sometimes I can't figure out what the hell she wants from me. What is it with you women?"

I shrug. Since I am not a woman who would want anything to do with him, I am not sure what a woman would want from him. My mind is numbly blank but I try to kick it back into gear, to keep the conversation going. I don't know why I am trying so hard. Not like I expect it to really make a difference in the end. Maybe it really is some curiosity about the inner workings of someone who seems like an alien to me.

"How long have you been together?"

The troll visibly relaxes, lets out a heavy sigh. I think he is starting to enjoy this conversation. It strikes me all as so bizarre, but what about this whole thing hasn't been bizarre.

"Eight years. We have a daughter. We're not married or nothing but she and Tammy, they're my family."

"Tammy's your daughter?" I try to picture what his offspring would look like. I hope for her sake, Tammy looks like her mother.

I reflexively flinch as he reaches behind his back. Expecting a gun to come out, instead, he pulls out his phone. He taps on the screen several times and then holds it up for me to look at. I don't want to get any closer to him but I am too far away to see the picture he is displaying. And he knows it so to not get closer would clearly show I really don't give a shit about any of this. But after all the effort thus far, it's silly not to keep going. So I step towards him as he does the same. My hair stands on end, the rush of adrenaline from fear that comes from standing near a man who can take my life at any moment. A man who has made it clear that his intent to cause harm.

I look down at the phone. A bright faced blonde haired smiling girl in a soccer uniform and pigtails. Okay, she is sort of cute. Maybe she's not his? I don't suggest this possibility.

"She's cute." I don't know what else to add to this. The part of the brain responsible for basic conversational skills is really being shut out by the more primal parts focused on simple survival.

"Thanks. She's a great kid." He slips the phone back into his pocket. He is beaming with a father's pride. Apparently it is a feeling felt even by those who are full of cruelty and ignorance. But try as I might, I can't ignore the knot in my stomach, the bile of hatred and anger in my throat and the pounding sense of fear in my brain. I can't reconcile the images so I fall silent. I can't do it. I can't pretend to be having a normal conversation with a fellow human being. None of it is true.

I look out the window as an awkward silence sets in, like a gap in a conversation at a cocktail party after you get past talking about the weather and sports and jobs.

The silence is broken as Davis comes around the corner.

"Dude, you better come see this. We've got trouble."

Chapter 44

My heart literally stops, I believe. I was the last one in there. Surely there was no trace of my activities. I did close the e-mail window, right? Suddenly I am not so sure and the world starts to spin as my mind starts to race. And what about the damn browsing history? Why hadn't I thought about that? Shit.

The troll grabs me roughly by the arm and drags me towards the room.

"Let's see what the problem is, dear." It is a sneering command, not an invitation.

He drops my arm as I come to a stop standing in front of the table of computer equipment. Davis looks like a perfectly in place geek with the glow of the screen creating a ghostly color to his face. The troll looks questioningly.

"Look man."

The troll circles behind the make shift desk and leans forward to get a good look at the screen. I swear my heart stops again and then starts racing at about one hundred and eighty. My palms sweat and my stomach churns. Somehow, I think my move is not going to be made at my leisure.

The troll pauses for a moment, processing what he is seeing.

Davis chimes in to clarify, eager to seem on top of things. "She sent an email, man. Warning someone about what was going on. We're fucked."

Almost without thought the primal brain kicks in and the fight for survival overcomes all other cognition. With a sudden surge of energy, I grab the edge of the plywood that is the tabletop and heave it up and forward. With a loud crack of glass and plastic, the whole table of equipment flies forward and down directly on top of Davis.

I hear a scream and a thud as he is literally buried under the pile of equipment. The troll is knocked backwards and slams into the wall, sliding down nearly to the ground.

I turn and break for the great room and the door to the backyard on the far side.

I don't make it far when the troll comes flying across the room, tackling me to the floor. I throw my arms up in a desperate attempt to break my fall and protect my head from the hard wood floor. My whole body throbs from the impact. The troll lands on top initially but slides off to the side.

I scramble on all fours trying to scoot away but he catches my ankle and drags me back. I kick wildly with my free leg but only land some glancing blows as his free arm acts like a brick wall bouncing my leg off like a wet noodle.

I roll over onto my back as he drags me under him. He straddles my hips, pinning my legs with his feet. My instinct for survival drives me on, swinging with my hands, trying to land a full blow to his face or stomach.

I suddenly stop short as he slides a very large and very sharp knife out of a sheath on his belt. He holds it up to my neck as I become perfectly still. I can feel the cold sharp edge resting on my throat just above my trachea. I am afraid to swallow lest the movement of my larynx cause the blade to slice into my skin. One quick slash with a knife like this would be my end.

The troll leans over me, smiling a grim smile.

"You have created a real mess, you know. Pretty sure the boss is gonna want to kill you now. So I am gonna have some fun first. Been wanting to do this since I first saw you."

I say nothing. Begging for my life seems pretty pointless as does any effort at an apology. All I can think to say is "Fuck you."

This just makes him laugh. "Yes, you will."

With a quick move, he pulls the knife away and wraps his left hand around my throat. The pressure threatens to cut off my airway completely. I squirm a little, but this only serves to make him tighten his grip. The room starts to spin a bit.

He places the knife on the floor next to his leg so he can use his free hand to loosen his belt.

Time seems to speed up and stand still all at the same time. I can't say my life flashes before my eyes. The thoughts are so much more primal than that. It is simply an overwhelming instinct to survive, no words, no true thoughts, just an overwhelming impulse.

I slide my left hand down slowly, trying to feel for the knife without alerting him to my movements. I cough a bit as his hand loosens, distracted with trying to focus on his pants. I feel the smooth wood handle at my fingertips. Stretching, I try to catch it, spinning it into my grasp. I am able to slide a bit that way as he rises up to position himself to work on my pants.

It is just enough for me to grab the handle of the knife. Without thought, without a plan, I plunge the knife into his right side at the level of the liver. It slides in effortlessly, just below the ribs.

His face freezes for a moment as his brain struggles to process this sudden turn of events. His hand instinctively grabs his side. I pull the knife back out and buck my hips up, punching him in the chest at the same moment. This serves to knock him backwards and sideways, allowing me to scoot out from under his weight.

He rocks back on his knees, a silent scream of pain pasted on his face. I start to scramble to my feet, the knife still poised in my left hand. The wound is serious but might not be fatal if he gets help right away. I'll call when I get to a phone, I think grimly to myself.

Although I am not sure why I care at the moment. Maybe decent moral people try to stay that way even in the worst of circumstances.

I have spent hours with a blade in my hand, wielding it with fine precision and well-honed skills. Never have I used it to destroy with such barbaric aggression. Life forces us to make choices we do not want to have to make.

Just as I get my feet under me, the troll seems to get a burst of anger-fueled adrenaline. He lunges forward and catches me around the knees. I fall roughly backwards, landing back on the floor with a thud. My head smacks the floor and the stars start to come out. But I don't let go of my death grip on the knife.

Please don't make me do this. I vaguely notice this thought go through my mind. But it is so fleeting as to be non-existent. The rage on his face triggers my last desperate instinct. I raise the blade. Grabbing it firmly in both hands, I plunge upwards and outwards aiming just to the left of center of his lower chest. The blade slices through skin and muscle, sliding past bone with little effort. The last tissue it penetrates is the thick muscular wall of the left ventricle.

I hold it there for a moment. The troll's eyes grow wide and he stares into mine.

"What did you do?"

With those final words, he falls sideways, landing on his side with a thud. The knife handle sticks out of his chest, the entire blade buried in his body. I scoot backwards on my hands and feet.

With one last gasping breath, the troll leaves this world, leaves my world.

I sit panting on the floor for a moment, trying to take in the events of the last minutes. Feeling like it was an hour, but it was just a few moments. My overwhelming urge is to curl up on the floor and cry.

Instead, I clamber to my feet. I don't know the status of Davis and really don't care at the moment. Other than the possibility he could come out of the room at any moment really pissed off.

So I quickly decide the best course of action is to run far and run fast.

Chapter 45

There is a reason for the expression, "Timing is everything." The moment you are delayed in line at the grocery store behind the elderly woman counting out her exact change makes you arrive a moment after the deadly collision. The shortcut gets you to the intersection just at the instant that the truck runs the red light. Time can change your life, it can save it and it can take it.

I discover the truth of this saying right now. A moment quicker and I would have made a clean getaway. Instead, a moment's hesitation puts me coming out of the doorway of the house just as Clean Cut pulls up the driveway.

Without thought I take off running across the lawn, heading for the woods next to the house. I can only hope and pray there is a neighbor not too far on the other side of the woods.

I hear Clean Cut yelling at me. Something about I better come back or I would be sorry. Somehow I think sorry is how I will end up if I go back.

I crash into the woods, small branches whipping me across the face and chest, briars catching on my jeans. A shot rings out. I duck instinctively as a piece of bark flies off a tree just above and ahead of me. I press on, keeping my head down, trying to pick an unobstructed pathway through the woods. None of this is done all that quickly or easily.

I can hear him crashing behind me, following me deeper into the woods. At least it is harder to get a clear shot in here with the dense tree stand creating cover. I have to hang a sharp left as I come straight up against a huge patch of dense blackberry bushes, beautiful but covered in deadly sharp thorns.

Unfortunately, this serves to put me a on a track of angling back towards where I came from and directly at Clean Cut. I probe desperately for a way through the thicket. It is so dense I can't even crash through ignoring the thorns.

Finally I come around the edge and the woods open up into a clearing. On the far side of the clearing, the tree line is thin, and I can see the chimney of a house through the canopy. I break into a full out sprint across the clearing. Both to get to the house quicker and to minimize my risk of being shot out in the open. My legs wobble with fear and exhaustion as I pray to not do a face plant in the middle of the field.

I hear heavy footsteps behind me but I dare not take the time to look back. But then everything comes to a crashing halt. Clean Cut comes at me with a flying tackle. I land hard on the rocky soil. The impact knocks all the wind out of me and I lay motionless, unable to fight, unable to even breathe.

Clean Cut stands up over me. I lie in his shadow. I want to scream but that requires air and all I can manage is a little groan. He grabs my hair and drags me to my feet. My legs feel like jelly, and I mostly stumble and am partly dragged back across the field and into the woods.

He doesn't say anything on the way back to the house. He never loosens his grip on my hair. I try to fight and pull away but it is like a two-year-old fighting with her father. Sadly pathetic and pointless.

I finally regain the ability to speak. "Please. Just stop. I can walk."

I need to slow everything down, regain some sense of control. Of my own body if nothing else at the moment.

After another stumble that brings me to my knees, he lets go of my hair. Grabbing my arm he pulls me back up to my feet. His face inches from mine, he growls, "I will kill you if you even think about running."

I nod feebly in submission. My mind is racing through all the events of the last minutes, desperately searching for a good outcome, a solution that doesn't end up with me dead. I can't find any place in my brain that allows for that.

We walk more civilly back across the lawn to the house. My stomach threatens to bring up whatever bile and little food may be down there. My ribs ache with each breath from being tackled by a two hundred pound gorilla. My skin burns from all the little scratches and scrapes picked up on my adventure through the woods.

I wish I could say I stop to think about Bode, think about if he is okay, if Mike made it to him, if Mike even bothered to go. But I don't. The fact of my imminent and immediate demise is all consuming.

Clean Cut leads me through the door. He pushes me to the floor and quickly handcuffs my right hand to the refrigerator. And here I was thinking the situation couldn't get worse. Now any chance of fighting or escape is pretty well gone. Hard to make a break for it with a Maytag on your arm.

He circles around the island in the kitchen. Up until that moment, the troll's lifeless body and pool of blood had been out of view. Clean Cut stops short, an indescribable look on his face. A combination of anger, disbelief, disgust, fear. He looks back at me, his expression unchanging. His brain frozen for a moment. I shrug. It seems like the only response I could give him.

He next goes down the hall and looks into the computer room. He disappears for a moment and then pops back out.

"Well, Doc, you've made a fucking mess. Your patient is still alive, but somehow I don't think you care about that."

I shrug again. Again, no more adequate response I can think of.

Clean Cut slips his cell phone out and hits a speed dial button.

"Hey. We're fucked. Everything is blown to hell."

He stops to listen for a moment.

"No. He's dead. Davis is out. Equipment is ruined. I can't salvage this fucking mess."

Again a pause during the response.

"Okay. Consider it done."

He ends the call and trades the phone in his hand for his Glock.

My mouth goes dry. I can't believe after everything, my life is going to end with me handcuffed to a refrigerator in the middle of God knows where, killed by some asshole who is doing some criminal activity that I have nothing to do with and no interest in interfering with. They can steal whatever they want, however they want to do it. I just wanted to, still want to, live. I think I am pretty much fucked on that one.

He walks over to me, gun aimed at my head. I keep my eyes glued to his, fighting the instinct to close them in an attempt to wish away the next moments.

"I really am sorry about this, Doc. It didn't have to be this way, but you had to get all cocky and think you could get away. Now you and your brother are going to die. I don't want to kill you, but you left me no choice."

Pleading for my life strikes me as quite pointless but the brain reflexively grasps for anything.

"You don't have to kill me. I'll walk away; never say a thing to anyone. I don't give a shit what you or your boss are up to. I'll just walk away, and you'll never see me or hear anything about me again. Please."

That's the best I can come up with. And it is all true. I don't give a shit. I would be happy to walk away with my life and let justice catch up with them in some other time or place or life.

"Can't do it Doc. I'm sure you understand that."

Not really, but there is no point in arguing. Now I close my eyes, waiting for the bang. Wondering if there will be enough time between the sound of the shot and the impact that rips through my brain to actually hear the shot.

A moment in time that seems like eternity.

The roar of a gunshot. I heard it. But I don't feel it. Am I dead so instantly that I am in another life and never felt the moment of death? No, that's not it.

I open my eyes. There is no bullet hole in my head. Instead, Clean Cut lies on the floor, a gaping bullet hole in his head. His eyes still wide open in surprise.

At the door, Mike lowers his gun as several other police officers pile in behind him, guns drawn.

Chapter 46

Save the various cuts, abrasion, bruises and aching muscles, I have suffered no major injuries. Mike tells me several times to go to the hospital. But that in itself would require a significant amount of explanation to people there and I don't have the energy for it. I argue with him until I win.

For the next argument he tries to get me to leave with one of the officers who is ready to drive me home. I can't leave. Not yet and I convince him to let me stay. I think he is actually pleased with it so that he can drive me home. I don't know why after everything, he would feel that way. And I am not sure why the idea is okay with me.

You would think I want nothing more than to get the hell away from the place. To leave the scene of carnage and destruction, fear and anger. Instead, I am drawn deeper into it. I can't take my eyes off of the troll, his grey blue corpse lying in a dark maroon pool of congealed blood. I did that. I took a knife, plunged it deep into a man's heart and took his life. The scene plays over and over. I can still feel the soft resistance, the quiet whooshing sound as the blade went in. The look of shock, uncertainty and fear in his face in that moment when he realized his own death.

The coroner eventually loads up the body, leaving just the dark stain on the floor. The floors will be scrubbed clean eventually but this house will always remember. There will forever be microscopic traces of this human being in the cracks and crevices. I finally turn away. There is no peace to be found there. Now I am regretting winning the argument with Mike about leaving. Maybe I shouldn't always try to take the hard way.

I wander around the house, reliving the hours I lived here, for a brief couple of days. Eventually I make my way into the computer room. Davis has long since been packed up by the rescue squad and carted off back to the hospital, back to where all of this began. The computer equipment lay in a heap on the floor. The crime scene unit is due to come in and start taking it all apart, carting it off to be analyzed and deciphered.

In the far corner of the room, on the floor, a tiny blinking green light catches my eye. I pick my way through the rubble towards it. Bending over, a knot forms in stomach, a lump in my throat. It is the troll's phone. It must have fallen out of his pocket when he went down under the computer equipment.

I know I shouldn't touch it. I should walk away. Point it out to someone. Ignore that I saw it. Anything but pick it up. But just as in the bar, when I throw myself into a fight with a guy twice my size, I do what I shouldn't. It's playing with fire, risking the ire of Mike and the entire crime scene unit. But like a moth to the flame, I can't stop. I crouch down. Hesitate for moment, my hand hovering over it. The steady blink of the green light seems to match the beating of my heart.

I pick it up, standing turned, to make sure no one can watch me from the door. Pressing the buttons, the screen comes to life. A new text message. The home screen picture, the grinning pig-tailed faced little girl. The text message from her. The last message from a daughter to her father. "Daddy I miss u. When ru coming home?"

My knees buckle a little. An impulse to cry but no tears seem to come. A sudden sense of rage, of blinding anger towards the troll. Why did he make me do it? Kill him? I didn't want to. I tried not to. I just wanted to live. I just wanted to be safe. And now a little girl will go to sleep wondering why her daddy has not answered. Why her daddy hasn't come home. Why her daddy will never come home.

Strangely I feel connected to her. A certain sense of responsibility for her. I impulsively scroll through his pictures, finding the one he showed me of Tammy. I tap to send it by text. I type in my cell phone number. Pausing for a second, wondering why I am doing this. But a sense of compulsion drives me forward. I click send. Now that picture can be mine forever. A reminder of the darkness we can all create in the moments of desperation. And lives are changed forever.

Chapter 47

Thankfully it is not too much longer before Mike is ready to go. The trip feels like it is forever and the physical exhaustion of no sleep and the emotional exhaustion of being on the edge for days starts to catch up with me.

The ride is mostly silent. The divide between us is palpable. At the same time, there also seems to be a mutual longing to find a way across the divide. But there is so much to say that there is nowhere to start. So neither of us try.

We discuss whether I should be at home alone. The possibility of his staying with me, or me going home with him is an option neither one of us wants to go near. So instead we settle on my going to stay with Michele. She had just gotten back into town and after a quick phone call, it is decided.

There is something to be said for having a best friend who is so close that you can walk in the door and fall apart and not feel uncomfortable or judged. That is what happens. I can no longer hold it all inside and it flows out in deep sobs. Michele simply sits on the couch, her arm around me. Her free hand supplying a steady stream of tissues.

After the great catharsis, I settle into a post cry exhaustion. Michele makes me a cup of nectarine ginger tea. The tangy fruity taste is smooth going down. Settles softly in my stomach. I realize I haven't eaten anything much for several days. Michele's mom instinct hits full overdrive and before long there is a plate with a grilled cheese sandwich and chips on my plate. And a chocolate chip cookie.

I smile weakly, gratefully. "Thanks Michele. You're the best friend a basket case could have."

Michele laughs, sits down on the couch next to me, pats her hand on my knee. "And you are the best basket case a girl can have."

I actually find a laugh. It seems to release the last emotions stuffed way down inside. Sometimes when your world has exploded and the emotional circuits are fried by the events, it turns to unexpected and inappropriate laughter. This is where I find myself. I laugh harder. "Man, I wish there was a little Jack D to add to this tea. I think I deserve it, don't you?"

Michele raises an eyebrow and gives me a "you've got to be kidding me look".

If I had made this comment to almost anyone else but Michele, there would be no big significance, no irony appreciated in it. But on Michele, the full weight of its meaning, the implication of an action like that is not lost.

With all of the attitude it deserves and just the right tinge of sarcasm Michele gives her reply. "Girlfriend. Don't you even dare. Cause I am not wiping your ass or listening to your crazy hallucinations of midgets playing in the hallways when you decide to climb back on the wagon and hit the DT's"

I burst out laughing. I don't remember a lot about my detox, when I went through delirium tremens as my brain learned to live life with alcohol. But the stories Michele told me, of crazy hallucinations, unfiltered expressions of emotions and just plain stupidness that was me are enough to make me laugh. For a long time I was ashamed, embarrassed about it. But with time, and the easy, accepting, loving way that is Michele, I saw the humor in it. The ridiculous way we can behave when the brain takes over the mind and everything spins out of control.

"Yeah, that was pretty embarrassing. You saw my naked ass."

Michele laughs now too. "Yeah, and you are so lucky it was me. You kept trying to show that ass to everyone in the unit. I definitely covered your ass."

This cracks us both up. The emotions turn into fits of laughter, ripples that go on for several minutes until we are both crying and holding our sides. Suddenly I have an impulse to hug her. I reach out and wrap my arms around her neck. She embraces me, holds me tight. The fear we have both carried since the breakout is felt in that hug.

As the hug ends, the laughter subsides as the reality of the last days sets back upon us.

I look away as a tear dislodges from my eye and rolls down my cheek. "I killed a man, Michele. I took a knife and I pushed it into his heart. And now his little girl has no father."

Michele grabs my hands, shakes them up and down a couple of times. "Hey now. Kate, look at me."

I feel like an ashamed child, I don't want to look at her but her gentle coaxing reminds me of the safe place I have with her. I turn my head back towards her. She looks intently in my eyes, her soft brown eyes dancing. "You did what you had to, Kate. You had no choice."

I sigh heavily. "I know you're right Michele. I can't explain it. He was a horrible man and was going to rape and kill me. But to know that another man has died at my hands...... It's a lot to process."

To her credit, Michele does not hone in on the fact I said another. I have no doubt she heard it and that someday soon we will have the discussion. After all, she has always proven to be the truest, safest place I have.

She puts her hand on my back and rubs up and down. Her natural gift is to comfort and to care for others and in this moment I appreciate it more than ever. "I can't imagine what you are going through, Kate. But I am so grateful that you are here to sit on my couch and feel badly about things. I wouldn't trade that for any man's life."

I give her a weak smile and wipe away the lingering tears. "Man, this has been a hell of a week. I'm sure it will get better with time and I can move on with life. It's just gonna take a while."

But even as I am saying it, I am not so confident of that truth. And the image of a little girl with pigtails flashes in my brain. I offer a silent prayer that both of us will find peace and healing.

Chapter 48

Mike picks me up in the morning to drive me up to see Bode. He insists on driving me. Maybe I let him because I am too tired to argue. Or maybe somewhere inside, I want to be with him. I want a way to see through all the hurt, the sense of betrayal. I am not sure if I can in the end. But for now, all I know is he has saved my life and more importantly Bode's life. I had trusted him and he did not fail me on this most important task. The connection is deep and permanent now even if we never find our way back to each other.

My plan is to see Bode. But there is someone else I need to see first.

A smile crosses his face as Samson is led into the visitation room and pointed in my direction. A flash of a memory. Another creepy smirk from another evil man. A chill runs through me but I fortify myself, drawing on anger to quiet any sense of intimidation.

He sits down. Folds his hands on the table. Soft hands, without calluses or scars. This is a man who does not do his own dirty work. We engage in a brief staring match. Neither blinks. But he speaks first.

"Hello Kate. It's nice to finally meet you."

I fold my hands and place them on the table, square my shoulders and lean forward. I will not bow before this man. "I can't really say the same."

"No, I would imagine you can't. You look well. Has life been kind to you?" A glint of mirth in his eyes.

Heat rises in my face. I cannot let him get to me. "If by kind you mean I am the last one standing, then yes, I would say kind."

He doesn't hide his amusement now. He is truly enjoying this conversation. It makes me doubt the wisdom of it. But I need answers to my questions, to put rest to my doubts. Although the doubt that this man will be truthful makes the accomplishment of that highly unlikely. Even with the answers I want to hear, there will always be that still small voice saying "what if…"

I clear my throat and continue. "I need to know the truth."

"Truth? About what, my dear?"

The use of this term of endearment fuels my anger. "I know what you did. I know you are behind everything that has happened to me in the last week."

Samson nods his head, encouraging me to go on.

"What I need to know is, did Bode know what was going on? Was he a part of this?"

Samson leans back, looks up at the ceiling for a moment. Looking back down, he gazes at me intently. "Why don't you ask him?"

"I'm asking you. After what you put me through, I at least deserve an answer from you."

"Oh Kate. How often in life do we really get what we deserve?"

"You'll never." I clench my hands. I feel the sweat as my fingers press down into my palms.

Another laugh. This time I smile back. A game of cat and mouse. I am determined to be the cat.

"Kate. I like you. I have great admiration for you."

"What the hell do you even know about me?"

"Oh, you'd be surprised."

"Oh, I don't know. Not much surprises me anymore. You haven't answered my question."

"Yes, was Bode involved? Do you really think he was? He is your brother. You have known him your whole life. Would that man, that boy you grew up with, risk your life?"

"No." I say it with a sense of conviction that surprises me.

"Well then, there you go."

Silence envelopes us as I sit with that answer for a moment. In some weird way, it is enough of an answer. I do know Bode. I know him enough to know he would never hurt me. I decide to choose to believe that. At least in this moment.

"Then why me? Just because?"

"Why not you?"

His answers consisting of questions is getting old. A flash of anger that I can't hold back. "Just tell the good damn truth for once in your miserable life. What the fuck do you want from me?"

His eyes narrow and his brow furrows. He leans in close over the table. "I want everything, Kate."

I lean back, protecting my personal space from his sudden invasion. "Why? What have I ever done to you?"

"Do you read your Bible, Kate? Have you ever heard the phrase 'the sins of the father'?"

"Yes."

Samson leans back, throws his hand out, palm up as if throwing an answer onto the table. "Then you know why."

"Quit with the damn games. What the hell are you talking about?" I am starting to feel like I am having a conversation with a demented patient. Two people talking but it is two separate conversations, one of which means absolutely nothing.

"Your father, Kate. He cost me a lot. He owes me. And with him gone, the debt passes to his children. I couldn't believe my luck when he showed up here to visit his son."

My mind is reeling by this point. My father? A man I just saw for the first time in years? A man who just died days ago? The puzzlement shows on my face. It gives Samson a sense of triumph, of having the upper hand. And I have to admit, at the moment he does.

"I understand how you could be confused. A man you haven't seen for years. A man you only know in distant memories and fading dreams. But he was much more than you know. He was a man whose conscience was much stronger than his greed. A man who had to do the right thing, even though it cost him dearly. The thing is Kate, he cost me even more. He cost me my freedom, my fortune, my reputation."

My brain scrambles to recall anything I may know about Samson. Not a lot. White-collar crime is what Bode said. His name seems vaguely familiar. I recall my father's warning. Even with all the missing pieces, the puzzle starts to take some form. "My father is the reason you are in prison." It is an educated guess.

Samson claps his hands quietly, slowly. "Bright girl. I knew you could figure it out. Your father and I worked together for a hedge fund. We were on the verge of making a fortune. We were bending the rules a little, but who wasn't? It was just information. I just happened to get it before the general public. There was no harm. But you father couldn't live with it. He turned me in, turned to the bottle and then disappeared before I could repay him for the favor."

Suddenly, all the resentment, the anger, the blame I held towards my father feels false, selfish, childish. I thought he was a weak man. A coward who couldn't leave the bottle, couldn't stand by his family. Was I wrong about all of it, some of it? So many secrets, even among those who share a home, who sit at dinner table every night. How can you ever really know someone?

"Well, he's dead now."

"So I have heard."

"Then just let it go. Why can't it just be over? Bode and I had nothing to do with it."

"I told you Kate, the sins of the father. Sometimes the innocents pay the price for the actions of another."

A stab of guilt. He has no idea how that truth cuts to my core.

"Well you used me, you terrified me, you will haunt my dreams forever. I can't prove you were involved. No one can with your thugs dead. You got away with it, all of it. Let that be the end."

Samson cocks his head, rolls his eyes up as if searching his own mind. "Hmm. It's tempting. Because I really do like you Kate. You have fight. You have an edge." He looks back down, eyes locked on mine. "Who knows what the future holds? Maybe someday you will wake up and find the debt has been paid in full. Or maybe you'll find that some more is still owed."

"Really? Really? Do you get off on fucking with people like this?" My exasperation with this whole conversation declares itself. It is clear I will not get any closure from this twisted dark soul of a man. I feel dirty just being in his presence. Like I need a long hot shower.

He is laughing now. Savoring his sense of triumph, of power.

I can't let him have that satisfaction. I lean forward, beckon him to lean in. In a low steady voice I share my final thoughts. "Power is an illusion. None of us can control life. None of us knows what tomorrow will bring. But I know that I will not let you win. I will live my life the way I want, love the people I want to love, and do good things in this world. All while you rot away in your little four by six cell. While you are savoring your one daily hour of sky, I will come and go where I please, when I please and enjoy every minute that I breathe the free air and feel the warm sunshine. I win. Because you have already lost."

Chapter 49

I step out to go to the restroom. After splashing water on my face, I start to feel cleaner, calmer. I try to shake the uneasiness left from the not veiled threat Samson shared. If he really is as powerful as Mike says, then how can I ever really be safe?

I push those thoughts to the back of my brain and focus on Bode. I realize that I am excited to see him and I hurry back to the visitation room to wait for him.

I break out into a broad grin as he is escorted in. I long to hug him and never let go, but we keep it brief before sitting down at the table.

"My God Kate, what the hell is or was going on? Some dude shows up here telling the warden that someone wants to kill me. Next thing I know, I get whisked off to segregation. No one would tell me anything."

"It's a long story, Bode. I am just so grateful you are okay."

In a quick synopsis I relay the events of the last days to him. His eyes grow wide at times, then narrow down in anger at other times. Relief finally wins out in the end as I sum up the story.

His face clouds with anger as he thinks through the story. "Samson set this whole thing up?"

"Yup. Crazy isn't it? All because of Dad."

Bode is silent, staring over my shoulder into space. He seems to be uncertain, unsure to say what he feels the need to say.

It is clear there is more but I refuse to believe he knew what Samson was doing. I go with that. "I know you weren't involved in all of this but you're holding back. Tell me. I deserve the truth." I am surprised by the sense of anger that rises up inside me. I can feel our relationship shifting, like all that it has been built on is turning out to be a little out of square, a bit unsteady.

He finds the courage to look me in the eyes. "I didn't know anything about it, Kate. I swear. But I did know..." His voice trails off.

Suddenly a light goes on in my brain. "You knew what? About Dad."

I can see the truth in his eyes. "Yeah, about him testifying against his business partner. That he left to protect all of us because he knew his partner wouldn't let it go. But I swear, I didn't know it was Samson who was the partner."

I can't quite identify the emotion. Hurt? Angry? Sad? "Why didn't you tell me?"

"You were a kid. You were so upset he left. He wanted you to hate him. He thought it would be easier. That it would keep you from trying to find him. He knew if you wanted to find him, you wouldn't quit until you did. And that would put you in danger too."

I ponder this. Despite all the years of anger, I know what he says is true. That is my Dad. He knew me because I am just like him, good and bad. A sadness overwhelms me. "I miss him."

Bode's sadness matches my own. "Yeah, me too."

We sit together with our sadness, a shared grief that connects on a level without words, without sounds. Bode finally breaks the mood. He is good at moving forward in life. I am the one who tends to get stuck.

"We can't change what happened. But I am curious, how did Mike find you?"

"Traced the IP address from the email I sent him. Went to a cell signal that he was able to locate. Smart fellow it turns out."

"What are you gonna do about him?'

"Do? What do you mean?"

"He saved both of our asses. We both owe him, but I suspect he would prefer the way you repay the debt." Bode cracks himself up.

My face darkens with the memory of the sense of betrayal. "That can't happen. Not after he accused both of us of being criminals."

"What do you expect, Kate? It had to be a tough position. The guy was doing his job."

"You're taking his side?"

"No. I'm just saying life isn't always as black and white as you want it to be. There has to be some room for grey. "

It's not what I want to hear. I want to nurse my righteous indignation, feed my sense of being wronged. But somewhere inside, I realize that he is right.

"Kate, no one can live up to the expectations you have of yourself and of them. We all fail. We all make bad choices. We all live with consequences. But if we lose each other in the fall out, if we let the mistakes tear us apart, that is the real mistake."

I can't help but laugh at his earnestness. "Well thank you Doctor Phil. Just how many self-help books have you read in here?"

He grins. "Too many. It's the state's low budget attempt at prisoner rehabilitation. What do you think?"

"I think you're a ding dong. But I love you anyway."

"I love you too sis. But what about Mike? Give him a chance, Kate. I can tell you like him." It's his turn to laugh, to poke fun.

"Really? Is it that obvious?"

"Um, yeah."

"I am such a crappy poker player." I hold my face in my hands. I am so weary from the emotions of the last days. But at the same time, have this vague sense of hope.

Bode grabs my hands, looks me in the eye, his face suddenly serious. "I mean it, Kate. Give yourself a chance to be happy. Give Mike a chance to bring you that."

A half smile on my face, I squeeze his hands with mine. "I'm not making any promises but maybe it is time. Maybe I can try."

Chapter 50

Mike is leaning up against the car watching the world pass by when I come out of the prison gate. I drink in the tall lean body. The touch of grey shows his experience in life but the fine wrinkles around his eyes show he still knows how to laugh. The emotional pain has not erased the physical attraction. The memory of how it felt to be in his arms. How much will I risk to get that back?

He stands up and clears his throat as I approach. Reflexively, or maybe instinctually, I open my arms to him, searching for the warmth, comfort and safety of his arms wrapped around me. I seem to be finding my answers as I go along.

He doesn't question. He just accepts me. We fit together well. He stands a few inches taller than me, but I can rest my head on his shoulder without standing on tiptoes. Like we are two pieces of a puzzle finally found to fit together.

After a long moment, I loosen my grip and lean back, searching for his lips. I am not disappointed as he bends his down to meet mine. Our souls touch out there in the parking lot of the regional prison. But somehow it seems our souls had already met many lifetimes ago.

After what seemed like an eternity and not nearly long enough, we break apart. A moment where our eyes meet, my heart opens just a little. This is what I want, if I have the courage to move past the fear, to offer forgiveness to him and to myself. I decide in this moment to find that courage, or at least spend the rest of my life fighting for it. There will be conversations, things to work through, trust to rebuild. It will take some work. But work is something I am good at.

Mike's deep voice cuts into my private thoughts. "Want to stop somewhere? Grab a drink and a bite to eat?"

I pause for a moment. I try to remember the last time I drove the trip from the prison back to home without a stop to sit at the bar. I can't even come up with an approximate date. I'm not sure if there ever was.

I cock my head up at Mike, a slight smile drawing across my face. "Nope. I'm good. Let's go home." One demon slayed for today. Tomorrow will be another battle.

The End

Or is it just the beginning…..

Elizabeth Cook lives in central Virginia with her four legged family members. Trained in family medicine, she works as a hospitalist physician. *Dirty Wounds* is her first novel.

Visit her website at www.docnovelist.com

Dirty Wounds